Nursing the Soldier's Heart

Merrillee Whren

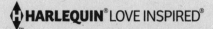

HARLEQUIN® LOVE INSPIRED®

Recycling programs
for this product may
not exist in your area.

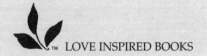 LOVE INSPIRED BOOKS

ISBN-13: 978-0-373-87977-9

Nursing the Soldier's Heart

Copyright © 2015 by Merrillee Whren

www.Harlequin.com

Printed in U.S.A.

"Brady, where are you?"

"In here." Funny how her voice quickened his pulse.

"Ready to go?" Kirsten poked her head through the doorway.

"Almost." As he gazed at her, he noticed the little blotch of blue paint on her cheek. Without thinking, he reached over and rubbed his thumb across it.

"You have paint on your cheek."

"I do?" Staring at him, she rubbed a hand across the place he'd touched.

His mind turned to mush, and all he could think about was spending more time with her.

"Mr. Brady, we're done," a little voice interrupted. Zach charged into the room and stopped abruptly, making Tyler nearly bump into his brother.

Brady smiled at the boys. "Would you guys like to grab a burger and meet Gram?"

The boys cheered.

"Am I invited, too?"

"Of course." Brady grinned. Things were definitely looking up. Kirsten had invited herself to join them.

Brady couldn't help thinking about the family picture the four of them presented.

Merrillee Whren is the winner of the 2003 Golden Heart Award presented by Romance Writers of America. She has also been the recipient of the RT Reviewers' Choice Best Book Award and the Maggie Award for Excellence. She is married to her own personal hero, her husband of thirty-five-plus years, and has two grown daughters. Please visit her website at merrilleewhren.com or connect with her on Facebook at facebook.com/merrilleewhren.author.

Listen to advice and accept discipline,
and at the end you will be counted among the wise.
Many are the plans in a person's heart,
but it is the Lord's purpose that prevails.
—*Proverbs* 19:20–21

I want to dedicate this book
to my granddaughters,
who remind me of what is important in life.

Chapter One

The familiar recorded voice on the other end of the line made Kirsten Bailey's stomach churn. The phone number had an Atlanta area code, but if it was a cell phone, no telling where the owner resided. She mustered some politeness and repeated her daily mantra. How many messages would she have to leave before she got a response? She slammed down the phone.

"Why are you abusing the phone?" Jen Chafin, the other late-shift nurse, swiveled in her chair as she tucked a lock of auburn hair behind one ear.

Kirsten grimaced. "Cora Barton asked me to call her grandson again. I've lost track of how many times I've left him a message. The man obviously doesn't care about his grandmother."

"Are you calling the right number?"

"Absolutely. The voice mail message says, 'This is Brady Hewitt. Leave a message.'" Kirsten shook her head again. "I hate the expression on Cora's face when I tell her I haven't reached him."

"Does he have a job where he's out of signal range for a period of time?"

"Cora doesn't know what he does." Kirsten shrugged.

"Sounds like he's a ne'er-do-well who picks up jobs here and there when he feels like it."

Jen turned back to her computer. "Does Cora have any other family?"

"I don't think so, otherwise I'm sure she would've asked me to call someone else. Her daughter died in a car accident when her grandson was young. Cora raised him."

Jen stopped typing. "That certainly makes him ungrateful."

"My thoughts exactly. How could someone ignore a grandmother like Cora? She's one of the sweetest women I know."

"Next time you could always leave a message telling him what you really think." Jen laughed halfheartedly.

"I'd like to, but I have to keep it professional." Kirsten grimaced. "At least Cora has lots of friends here at The Village to make up for her inattentive grandson."

Jen nodded. "And speaking of friends, look who's coming down the hall."

Kirsten peered over the counter. "Annie and her kids. That'll make Cora's day."

Kirsten waved at Annie Payton and her two small children, Kara and Spencer. The kids let go of their mother's hand and raced to the nurses' station.

Shaking her head, Annie caught up to her children. "Sorry, Kirsten. They're excited to see you."

"That's okay." Kirsten greeted the youngsters with a hug. "Who are you here to see?"

"Ms. Cora," the children said in unison.

"We want her to get better, and Mommy says our visits will help." Kara scrunched up her little nose. "I hope Ms. Cora gets out of here soon."

"We all do." Kirsten turned her attention to Annie. "How are the wedding plans?"

Annie's face brightened. "Everything's falling into place. Just ten more days."

Kirsten came around the counter and gave Annie a hug. "I'm so happy for you and Ian."

"Thanks." Annie glanced down the hallway. "Guess we better get down to see Cora. Talk to you later."

Kirsten waved as the trio went down the hallway. Seeing Annie and her children made Kirsten long for the family she'd almost had. But she shouldn't dwell on what could have been. She had to concentrate on the here and now.

"Are you going with someone to Annie and Ian's wedding?" Jen asked when Kirsten returned to her computer.

Kirsten frowned. "That's another sore topic."

"Really?"

"Yes. Maybe we should work and not talk at all."

"But I can work and talk at the same time." Jen waved a hand over the computer keyboard. "You know the rest of the evening is usually pretty quiet. Besides, you can't leave me hanging like this."

Shaking her head, Kirsten looked straight ahead as she input some data. "No fair. You have a husband who's a built-in date for such occasions, so you don't have to worry about someone trying to find you an escort."

"Your dad?"

Kirsten released a harsh breath. "Yeah. Ever since I came back from Brazil, he's been pushing some guy at me. I think he's hoping I'll find someone here, so I won't go back."

Jen nodded. "I can understand that. Lauren's a college senior, and I'm hoping she finds a job close to home when she graduates. I can't imagine what it would be like to have a child in another country, where you could never see them. Look at it from your dad's point of view."

Kirsten shrugged. "I suppose. Family's important to me. That's why I came home as soon as I found out how sick Mom was, and I stayed even after she passed away because Dad needed me. But he needs to let me live my own life, and he needs to get on with his."

"I'm sure the loss of your mom still weighs on him."

"I know. It hasn't been easy for either of us." Kirsten stopped typing and looked at Jen. "His duties as director here at The Village keep him busy, and that's good. But the nights are hard for him. He didn't want me to move into my own place, but I think that's better for him, don't you?"

"Probably, but your dad still looks at you as his little girl. You're an adult, but you're also his child." Jen grabbed a folder from the end of the desk. "He wants the best for you."

"I know that, but I wanted to adopt those three children in Brazil. Now that won't happen." Kirsten fingered the beaded bracelet on her wrist—the one Luciana, Nathalia and Rafael had made for her right before she came back to the States.

"Do you think they'll lift the suspension of international adoptions?"

"Those children are lost to me. But I'm still trying to get a new visa in order to go back." Kirsten tried not to think of those sweet children, but the image of their smiles and dark brown eyes looking up at her wouldn't go away. Losing them was worse than the day she'd found out she could never have children of her own.

"What about trying to adopt children here?"

"Another thing my dad suggests when I mention going back to my missionary work, but it's not the same. The kids here at The Village have wonderful homes with house parents who love them. The children in Brazil are in crowded orphanages with an inadequate number of caregivers. And there are many more on the streets." Kirsten tried to shake away the sad memories. "I love my dad and want to be here for him, but he has to move on with his life. So do I. Going back to Brazil is my plan. That's what I want more than anything."

"Even though the kids in the children's homes here have a wonderful place to live, don't you think the ones who are eligible for adoption would want a special family of their own?"

Kirsten shook her head. "I only know the children I worked with in Brazil were destitute and neglected far too often."

"Do you ever think these things happened because God has another plan for your life?"

Kirsten didn't want to answer that question. "For the ten years I was in Brazil, I knew God wanted me there. I want to go back."

"Think of it this way. You're still helping—helping your dad and these seniors who need your gentle caring spirit in their lives."

"I'm not sure my spirit is so gentle." Kirsten tried to smile. "Tracking down wayward grandsons and shoveling pills at senior citizens isn't exactly what I'd hoped to be doing with my life."

Forcing herself not to dwell on Jen's assessment of the situation, Kirsten grabbed some more charts and prayed for an uneventful evening. Were Jen and her dad right? Should she think about adopting children here? If she did that, how could she ever go back to Brazil? Why wouldn't God want her to return to Brazil as a missionary nurse? What better plan could He have for her?

After Kirsten finished her paperwork, she got up and checked the medication cart, then turned to Jen. "I've got a few meds to deliver, and I'll have to give Cora the bad news."

Jen shook her head. "I hope the unresponsiveness of her grandson doesn't affect Cora's recovery."

"Me, too. I hate giving her distressing news." Kirsten headed down the hall.

As she delivered the medications to her elderly patients, she willed herself to get rid of her negative attitude toward Cora's grandson. It would do Cora no good.

Four doors down the hall Kirsten came to Cora's room. The door was slightly ajar. A television blared with the local news.

Kirsten peered through the small opening. While Cora's roommate watched the television, Cora appeared to be sleeping. Not wanting to disturb her, Kirsten backed away, but she caught sight of a man with a scruffy appearance sitting in the chair at the foot of Cora's bed.

Who was he, and what was he doing there while Cora slept? Kirsten's radar for trouble zoomed into action.

Brady sat on the chair at the foot of his grandmother's bed and glanced around the room. What would he find here at The Village of Hope? His grandmother had come to live here after she'd had a slight stroke about four years ago. He'd prayed this place a good home for her.

At the time, he'd been in the army over in Afghanistan. There had been no chance to get home to see her. He shouldn't use that as an excuse because even when he'd been stateside, he'd never taken the opportunity to spend time with the person who'd saved him from foster care. He'd never appreciated that until now. He should've come to see her rather than calling her a few times a year.

Guilt for the years he'd stayed away consumed his thoughts. The time had come to make amends—to renew his relationship with the one person on this earth who actually cared about him. She looked so frail lying there, her gnarled fingers resting on top of the blanket. What had happened to the robust woman of his childhood?

Was she okay? Her eyes were still closed and she didn't move a muscle, but the steady rise and fall of her chest eased his mind. Her glasses and her well-worn Bible lay on the table next to the bed. She used to read that Bible every day and had gone to church every Sunday. He'd disregarded her faith—even mocked it. He was sorry about that, too.

So many of the decisions he'd made had been made with only a thought to his own life. Could he break that pattern? It might not be easy, but the time had come for him to think about someone besides himself.

Brady's stomach rumbled, and he glanced out the window at the tall pines interspersed with oaks and maples with leaves that held a hint of fall color. He wished he'd stopped to eat, but he'd wanted to get here before the place closed to visitors. Did they have a cafeteria where he could get supper, or a vending machine? If he went searching, he might run into the disagreeable nurse who had left far too many messages on his voice mail. Shaking his head, he smiled at his ridiculous thoughts. Why was he afraid to face this unknown woman of the numerous phone calls?

He was done hiding out in his grandmother's room. He would march out there and let the nurse know he was here. Brady Hewitt—soldier, oil-rig worker, commercial fisherman and all-around good guy. That last part was a stretch, but he was working on the good-guy stuff.

Pushing out of the chair, Brady looked toward the

door. A nurse stood in the doorway. Their gazes met. Her chocolate-brown eyes held him captive, and he couldn't look away. He fought to keep his mouth from dropping open. Did this attractive woman belong to the impersonal voice he'd heard over and over on his phone? Maybe she wasn't the nurse who'd called. He could hope. He hated to think that such a pretty face served as a facade for those unpleasant messages.

"Sir, may I speak with you out here in the hall?" The nurse motioned with her hand.

Nodding, Brady sauntered across the room to the door. He couldn't mistake the voice. The frosty tones on his phone's voice-mail messages belonged to the attractive nurse. He followed the nurse, whose dark hair was pulled into a knot at the back of her head. "What can I do for you, ma'am?"

Although she wasn't short, she had to look up at him. "Do you mind telling me why you're in this room?"

"Cora Barton is my grandmother. Is there a problem?" He feigned an innocent expression along with a smile as he rubbed his stubble-covered chin.

His height advantage didn't intimidate her as her dark eyes seemed to bore into his soul. She frowned. "So you're Brady Hewitt. I've been trying to reach you for days. Make that weeks. Why didn't you tell us when you arrived? Why didn't you answer my calls?"

"So you're Kirsten Bailey. Nice to meet you, too." He broadened his smile into a grin. Could he make her smile? She was the beauty and the beast rolled into one. Prickly and pretty all at the same time. Or maybe she was the beauty, and he was the beast. His disheveled looks might put him in that category. Was she going to chastise him? "Yes, I'm Brady Hewitt, and I arrived a few minutes ago. I know you've been trying to reach me."

"At least you could've told us you were coming, so I wouldn't have kept calling."

He'd lived on the edge for most of his life. He liked a challenge, and he could sense she was going to be one. "You know after listening to dozens of your messages, I figured I wasn't really interested in talking to you. But now that I'm here I'll let you know what I think."

"And what would that be?" Kirsten gave him a defiant look.

She wasn't backing down, and he liked that. But he wasn't going to back down, either. "You need to work on your bedside manner, Kirsten. Is it okay if I call you Kirsten?"

Blinking, she opened her mouth as if she was going to say something, then closed it without uttering a word. She stared at him as if she couldn't believe what he'd said. Okay, then. She obviously didn't have a sense of humor, either. Now what?

They stood there staring at each other until Kirsten finally blinked. "We have rules here, very strict rules about people coming and going."

Brady gave her a lazy grin. "Ma'am, I apologize if I broke your rules, but my name was on the list at the guardhouse at the main entrance, and the lady at the front door here had my name, as well. She buzzed me right in."

"But didn't she tell you to check at the nurses' station for Cora's room number?"

"She did, but on my way in, I met, ah… Annie was her name. She had two cute kids with her. The little girl was quite talkative and said they'd been visiting my grandmother. They gave me her room number and directions to get here." Brady could tell by Kirsten's expression she didn't have a response for his explanation. He took some pleasure in knowing he had her tongue-tied. "So you see I had no reason to check at the nurse's station."

Tight-lipped, Kirsten nodded. "Please remember in the future to let us know you're here. For security reasons, we like to know who's in the building."

"Yes, ma'am. I'll be glad to check in with you." Brady saluted, hoping to get a smile out of her, but none appeared. "Since Cora's sleeping, is there some place where I can get something to eat?"

"Follow me." Kirsten turned on her heel and proceeded down the hall.

Brady followed. He'd better behave himself because he'd sure hate to further annoy the pretty nurse. His haggard appearance wasn't going to win him any accolades. Nearly twelve hours of driving could take a toll on anyone's looks. And he had to remember this wasn't all about him.

When she reached the nurses' station, she stopped and turned in his direction. "Let me introduce you to the other late-shift nurse, Jen Chafin. Jen, this is Brady Hewitt, Cora's grandson."

The other nurse, who was older and a little on the plump side but with a much friendlier demeanor, came out from behind the counter and extended her hand to him. "Hello, Mr. Hewitt. So glad you're finally here."

Brady shook her hand. "Nice to meet you, Jen. Please call me Brady since I'll be hanging around here as long as Cora's here."

"She's a dear. We love her, but we're eager for her to make a complete recovery and get back in her apartment." Jen smiled.

He was glad to see his grandmother had loads of friends, who, unlike him, had been there for her when she needed help. "Is there a chance she could lose her spot in the assisted living center?"

Jen shook her head. "Not unless the doctor believes she needs to stay here, but that's not likely. She's making good progress."

Brady nodded. "Good."

Kirsten stepped behind the counter. "Brady would like something to eat. Should we send him to the cafeteria?"

Jen glanced at the clock, then back at him. "If you hurry, you might find the cafeteria open. Turn left down this hallway and go through the double doors. Signs should direct you. If they've closed down, you can still get something from the vending machines there. You're welcome to bring your food back to Cora's room."

"Thanks." Brady headed in the direction Jen had indicated, but stopped and looked over the counter at Kirsten. "Kirsten, I appreciate you letting me know about Cora. Have a good evening."

Brady didn't wait for a response because he probably wasn't going to get one. He was going to enjoy getting to know the by-the-rules nurse and see whether he could get past her defenses. A kind word was a better approach than his earlier criticism.

Besides having to soothe the ruffled feathers of the pretty nurse, he had to figure out what he was going to do now that he was back in Georgia. He'd rather be someplace less crowded—someplace with lots of space to breath—but he'd been thinking about his own wants for too long. The time had come to put his grandmother first. That meant finding a permanent job and a place to live here. He wasn't quite sure where that would lead him. Figuring it out was his first priority, not the attractive woman whose disdain challenged him to change her mind.

But he intended to put his charm into full gear.

* * *

"Now there's a fine-looking man, wouldn't you agree?" Jen leaned on the counter.

Kirsten shook her head. "If you like tattoos and the scruffy, unshaven look."

"I was concentrating on those golden-brown eyes and that tousled brown hair."

Shaking her head, Kirsten frowned. "He looks like he's been sleeping in his clothes, and that tousled brown hair hasn't seen a barber in weeks."

"Looks good on his six-foot-plus muscled frame." Jen let out a low whistle. "I think somebody needs an attitude adjustment."

"I suppose you mean me."

"Uh, yeah."

Kirsten sighed as Jen came back around the counter. "I know I was rude, but he made me angry. He was impolite not to let us know he was coming or that he'd arrived."

"Did he tell you why he never responded to your messages?"

Kirsten lowered her head and put a hand to her forehead. "He implied my messages were curt and unfriendly."

Shrugging, Jen frowned. "I thought you sounded okay when you left messages."

"Yeah, but you didn't hear them all. Maybe my anger came through even when I was trying not to let it show." Kirsten raised her head. "Oh well, he's here now, so I don't have to worry about it. I hope his presence will make Cora happy. That's all I care about."

An unsettled feeling washed over Kirsten as she tried to concentrate on her work. She didn't want to spend time defending her reaction to the smooth Mr. Hewitt. The man had waltzed in here thinking he could flash around his good looks and charm and make everything okay. Nothing about a cocky guy appealed to her, especially one with a plethora of military and animal tattoos decorating his arms. She suspected there were probably more that couldn't be seen.

Jen raised her eyebrows. "Did Cora seem happy to see him?"

"Don't know." Kirsten shrugged. "She was sleeping, and he was sitting there beside her bed when I looked into the room. All that matters is Cora's happiness."

"You're right." Jen nodded. "But I was thinking he might be a good candidate for your date to Annie and Ian's wedding."

With incredulity screaming through her mind, Kirsten turned to Jen. "You're joking, right?"

"No, I'm as serious as can be." Jen tapped her fingers on her keyboard. "Taking Brady would show your dad you can get your own dates."

"My dad would have a fit if I showed up with a guy sporting tattoos."

"And the plot thickens."

Kirsten shook her head. "There's no plot, and the only thickness is in your skull."

They worked for several minutes in silence until Jen craned her neck to see down the hallway. She chuckled. "The hero of our story is on his way back."

"Will you please behave?" Waving a hand at Jen, Kirsten stared at the computer monitor and hoped the man would pass by without a comment. "Don't say a word to him."

"Can't be unfriendly."

"We have work to do." Kirsten tried to concentrate on the scheduling chart on her monitor and to not be tempted to see where Brady was. Why was she letting him bother

her? She had to admit Jen was right. Underneath the tattoos and scruffy appearance was a good-looking man, but she couldn't let that interest her. Charm and good looks didn't undo bad character. What kind of man would ignore his grandmother for years?

"Hello, ladies. Care to share some of my contraband?" Brady held up a plastic bag bulging with unseen goodies. "I caught some of the cafeteria workers before they'd completely closed down. They loaded me up with treats."

"No, thanks. We've already eaten." Kirsten berated herself for not following her own advice. She had engaged the man in conversation. Now she'd have to pay the price.

Jen cast Kirsten a quizzical look, then smiled up at Brady. "She's not speaking for me. Let's see what you've got."

"Sure." Brady set a large drink on the counter, then proceeded to take several plastic containers out of the bag. "Roast beef. Gravy and mashed potatoes. Corn on the cob. Chocolate cake."

Jen stood and surveyed Brady's bounty. "How did you manage to get all this?"

Brady grinned. "I used my considerable charm on the ladies."

With her gaze downcast, Kirsten rolled her eyes. Besides being ill-mannered, this guy was full of himself, too. Hardly a captivating combination. But who was she to judge? She'd been rude, too. The urge to apologize sifted through her mind, but she couldn't find the words and quickly dismissed any desire to join the conversation.

Kirsten recognized that it wasn't just Brady's unresponsive behavior toward Cora that bugged her. He reminded her of Lance Tucker, the man who'd broken her heart in college. A charmer just like Brady, Lance had convinced her that he loved her. In the end, though, he'd broken her heart. She'd gone to his apartment unannounced and found him with another woman.

Jen nodded. "Looks like you used your charm well."

"There's more. I helped myself to the vending machine, too." Brady dumped several bags of junk food onto the counter. He picked up one bag and held it up. "I haven't had pork rinds in a long time."

"Not my favorite snack." Jen wrinkled her nose. "On second thought, Kirsten's right. We've already eaten so I'd better refrain from eating more, but you must be hungry."

Don't you have a grandmother to see? Kirsten wanted to ask him the question, but she pressed her lips together to enforce her own silence.

"Yeah, my stomach's been growling since I hit Interstate 285. I would've stopped to get something, but I wanted to get here." Brady split open the bag of pork rinds and popped one into his mouth.

"How far did you drive today?" Jen asked.

Brady swallowed. "Too far. Started out in Dallas this morning."

"Wow! You've driven a long way. You must've been eager to visit Cora."

Brady nodded and gathered his haul. "And I'd better get down there and see if she's awake."

As he sauntered down the hall, the bag swinging by his side, Kirsten couldn't help but look. She watched him until he disappeared into Cora's room. Aggravated with herself, she turned to find Jen grinning. "Okay, so you're right. He is good-looking."

"Aha. So are you going to ask him to the wedding?"

Frowning, Kirsten narrowed her gaze. "Absolutely not. I just met the man. What would he think if I asked him to a wedding when he barely knows me or anyone here?"

"He'd think his abundant charm had wooed you." Jen laughed.

Kirsten shook her head. "Maybe I'll take Dad up on one of his date suggestions just to put an end to this discussion."

Jen tapped a finger on her head. "Oh, good thought. Make the new guy jealous."

"You're impossible." Kirsten pressed a button on her keyboard and the nearby printer sprang to life. "I have reports to prepare. These days registered nurses spend more time filling in charts and reports than they spend with patients."

"I agree with you there." Jen lifted her own stack of papers and resumed her spot at the desk.

Kirsten grabbed the pages from the printer and pinned the schedule to the bulletin board, then sent an email copy to the nurse's assistants and LPNs. While she checked the next scheduled doses of medications, she tried not to think of Brady, but the image of his broad shoulders and disarming grin flitted through her mind. Despite his appeal, too many things about him said *bad boy*. She'd already dealt with one of those, and she didn't want to repeat the experience. Brady Hewitt was everything she didn't want in a man.

Chapter Two

Cora's roommate still had the TV near full volume when Brady returned to the room. His grandmother continued to sleep. A soft snore accompanied her breathing. How she slept through the noise was a mystery to him. He settled in the nearby chair, put his bag on Cora's rolling tray and extracted his food. As he opened the containers, the aroma made his stomach growl again. He grabbed the plastic fork and ate with abandon.

He scarfed down the food so fast he forgot to savor it, and he'd forgotten to thank the Lord for his blessings. He put down his fork and bowed his head. *Thank You, Lord, for bringing me safely here. Thank You for being with Cora and helping her to recover completely. And thanks for this food.*

When Brady raised his head, Cora was sitting up in bed. "Brady, is that you?"

"Gram, you're awake." Brady jumped up from the chair, put his food aside and hurried to her bedside. He gave her frail shoulders a big hug. "I finally got your message and came as soon as I could."

"Let me look at you." Cora eyed him from head to toe. "You've grown up a lot since I last laid eyes on you.

The pictures you sent don't do you justice. You look a lot like your dad."

Brady merely nodded. He didn't want to be anything like his dad. Brady hadn't seen the man in years. He'd made a promise to himself that he would make something of his life, not let his circumstances determine the outcome of his life as his dad had done.

"Why did it take you so long to get here?"

Hoping to avoid answering her question, Brady shoved the cart over to Cora's bedside. "You want something to eat?"

Cora waved a hand at him. "No, they feed us dinner around five o'clock. Can't eat another bite." She peered at the cart. "Is that chocolate cake?"

He chuckled. "I thought you said you couldn't eat another bite."

"There's always room for chocolate."

Brady slid the cake closer to Cora. "It's all yours."

"We can share, but I don't have a fork." Cora reached for her call button. "I'll page the nurse."

Brady took a deep breath. Would that bring Kirsten their way? Probably not. Registered nurses didn't usually bring forks to patients. Minutes later, his supposition proved to be true when a petite young blonde scurried into the room.

The young woman surveyed the room. "May I help someone in here?"

"I need a fork, so I can eat this delicious cake. And I want you to meet my grandson, Brady." Cora waved the young nurse's aide over. "Brady, meet Kayla. She takes really good care of me."

"Your grandma is super. Everyone here loves her." Kayla shook Brady's hand. "I'm so glad to meet you. Cora talks about you all the time."

That was the second time he'd heard the same thing today. "Thanks for taking good care of her, Kayla."

"It's a pleasure. I'll be right back with that fork." Kayla hurried away.

"Seems you have quite a fan club here."

Cora waved both hands at him. "The nurses here love everyone. They're so caring, but I still want to get out of here and back into my own place."

"I'm sure you do." Brady sat down again as Kayla returned with a fork.

Cora thanked the nurse's aide, then turned to Brady. "Now you can answer my question."

"You mean why it took me so long to get here?"

Cora nodded. "I had them calling you every day."

So that's why he'd had so many messages. Maybe he'd been a little too hard on Kirsten. "I know. When I retrieved my phone, I heard them all."

"Retrieved your phone?"

Brady scooted the chair closer to the bed. "I went up to Alaska this past May—"

"Alaska? You never told me."

Nodding, Brady grimaced. "I know. I haven't been good about staying in contact with you, and I promise I'll do better in the future."

"So why were you there?"

"I hired on as a deckhand on a commercial fishing boat during salmon season. Good pay." Brady reached over and took Cora's hand. "Gram, I would've been here sooner, but when they called I was in the middle of the sea. I got my messages when I retrieved my phone on the mainland."

Cora smiled. "I knew something wasn't right when you didn't return the calls."

"I got on the first flight out of Anchorage into Dallas.

My pickup truck was there because I'd planned to return to Texas when the summer fishing season was over."

"And you drove from Dallas today?"

Brady nodded. "Twelve hours."

"You must be exhausted."

"But seeing you has made the long trip worth it."

"And seeing you has made my day, my whole year. I was afraid I would never lay eyes on you again."

Brady hung his head. He wasn't good at saying he was sorry, but he was. Cora had aged, and he had to face the fact that the time he had left with her was limited. He'd missed too many years with her. How could he ever make up for that? "I'm here now. So let's make the most of it."

"After you got out of the army, I didn't hear much from you. You wrote a couple of times, but you never told me anything of significance about your life. I prayed for you every day while you were in the army *and* every day after you got out."

"Thanks, Gram. Your prayers saved me more than once." Not only from enemy bombs and bullets, but also from his own self-destructive behavior.

Her prayers had led him to Chaplain Howard, who'd urged Brady to take another look at Christianity. He'd remembered the Bible lessons from his youth and his grandmother's devotion to God. With the Lord's help, Brady stopped drinking to excess, misusing women and destroying his life. He'd spent the years since getting out of the army roaming from place to place, trying to find out where he belonged.

As Brady recounted the years since he'd been gone, he recognized the pattern—moving from one place to another, never finding a place to call home. Maybe he was more like his dad than he realized. The army had given him the discipline he'd lacked, and Chaplain Howard had capped that discipline with a moral code, but the army had also contributed to his wanderlust.

Now Brady wondered where the Lord was leading him. Did he belong here? He'd left his grandmother's house in anger when he'd been barely seventeen, vowing never to return. This was one of the last places he would have picked to settle down, but his grandmother and the challenge of getting a pretty but petulant nurse to like him invited him to stay.

"What are your plans?" Cora peered at him through the large glasses that covered a significant portion of her wrinkled face.

Brady didn't want to make any promises he couldn't keep. Staying here to help his grandmother was something he should do, but the thought of living in Georgia again didn't appeal to him. Finding a job was the only way he could stay, but he didn't have to make any decisions now. "I don't know, Gram."

"I wish you'd settle here. You're the only close family I have left."

"I'm going to have to figure that out." More guilt. He'd been gone for nearly twelve years, only visiting Cora twice during that time. He should've made more of an effort to be part of his grandmother's life.

After leaving on bad terms, he hadn't known how to make it right. The visits had always seemed uncomfortable. Cora had already been a widow when his mom, Cora's only child, had died in a car accident. After that his dad had gone into a deep depression and never recovered. That's when Cora had taken Brady in. She'd done her best to give him a decent life, but he'd done his best to make life difficult for her. Could he ever make it right?

"I can hardly wait to get out of here. I don't mind being in the assisted-living apartment, but I'll go crazy if they keep me in here." Cora's green eyes grew bright with tears as she grasped his arm. "You have to be my advocate."

Brady furrowed his eyebrows. "You mean, like having a medical power of attorney?"

"Yes, that's what it's called."

"But I thought that was for people who were dying or something." Brady's stomach sank. "You're not dying, are you?"

Cora chuckled. "No. Nothing like that, but I want you to be able to talk to the doctors and nurses about my medical issues. Sometimes, I'm not sure what the doctors are telling me. So I'd like to have you know what's going on, too. All that privacy stuff makes it so they can't talk to you unless I say so."

"What do I need to do?"

"Talk to the nursing home administrator, Ian Montgomery. He's a lawyer, too. I'm sure he'll know exactly what's required."

"Where do I find this administrator?"

"He has an office in the main building near the front gate." Cora waved one hand toward the door. "But you'd better do it soon. He's getting married in ten days. Then he'll be gone on his honeymoon."

Brady nodded. "I'll do it tomorrow."

"Good, because I want out of here so I can go to Ian and Annie's wedding. In fact, if they don't let me out, I'll escape."

"Gram, you aren't in jail."

"Well, it sure seems like it."

"I heard that. They'll be no escaping."

The familiar voice made Brady turn toward the door. He wasn't sure what to say as Kirsten pushed a cart into the room.

"Kirsten, have you met my grandson?" Cora saved him from having to say a thing.

Kirsten nodded. "We met earlier when he was looking for something to eat."

Cora looked at Brady. "She's the one who was calling you."

Brady gave Kirsten a wry smile. "Yeah, I know."

When Kirsten returned his smile, he almost fell out of his chair. Had the touchy nurse suddenly become friendly? There was a hint of humor behind her prickles. Maybe he had her wrong. She'd only done what his grandmother had asked.

Kirsten brought a little cup to Cora's bedside. "Time for your pain medication."

Cora frowned. "Do I need that stuff?"

Kirsten waved a finger at Cora. "You know if you don't take it now, you'll be waking up in the middle of the night in pain."

Cora poured herself a glass of water, then took the little cup. "I hate taking these pills."

"Gram, you need to stay ahead of the pain. You'll get better much sooner if you do."

"Listen to your grandson. He's right." Kirsten retrieved the empty cup after Cora took her medications. "And as for going to the wedding. If you work hard at your therapy and can walk the entire corridor with your walker, you can attend the wedding."

"And the reception, too."

Kirsten hesitated. "Why don't we leave that decision up to the doctor and the physical therapist?"

"But you'll put in a good word for me, right?"

Shaking her head, Kirsten laughed. "No promises from this corner. You have ten days to improve."

Cora released a heavy sigh. "That therapist is a slave driver."

"That's because she's on your side. She wants to help you get out of here, so you don't have to plan an escape." Kirsten looked at Brady. "I hope you're not assisting in any way with her intention to break out of here."

Brady held up his hands, trying to hide a smirk. "Not me. I wouldn't dream of it."

"I don't know why that doesn't comfort me." Kirsten took hold of the cart. "Take care, Cora. I'm off to finish delivering these meds."

As Kirsten wheeled the cart into the hallway, Brady looked over at Cora. "I'll be back in a minute. I want to ask her something."

"Out for a date?" Cora's eyes twinkled.

Brady frowned at her. "I'll pretend I didn't hear that."

"You should think about it," Cora called after him.

Brady stepped into the hallway, hoping Kirsten hadn't heard his grandmother's remark. A date. He could barely remember the last time he'd been on one. Or maybe he'd chosen not to remember because it had probably been a drunken one-night stand. He didn't want to remember those. Since he'd discovered his newfound faith in God, he'd been too busy working on oil rigs or catching salmon to bother with dates.

Besides, he doubted a date with Kirsten would be that great, or would it? He liked challenges. He liked adventure. He liked pretty women, even if they were a little on the hypersensitive side. What was he thinking? He'd only met the woman a half hour ago. She was likely to turn him down if he asked, but give him a few days and she would look at him through a different lens. That was the plan.

He looked both ways down the hall but didn't see

Kirsten. She'd probably already gone into another room. He stood there for a moment, and she reappeared. "Hey, Kirsten."

She turned, a little frown puckering her eyebrows. "Yes?"

He went down the hallway in her direction. "You have a minute to talk?"

She hesitated. "Not now. If there's something you'd like to discuss, I can do it after I finish delivering the meds. I can stop by Cora's room after I'm done."

"Sure." Brady watched her push the cart to the next room and forced himself not to think of her as just another attractive woman who'd caught his eye.

For a few minutes he leaned against the wall in the hallway and took in the sights and sounds of the place. He tried to put himself in Cora's shoes. Everything was clean and the nurses and assistants seemed very attentive to the patients here. But there was no denying the place had the feel and smell of a nursing home—a place from which patients often didn't go home. Was that what was worrying his grandmother? He supposed Kirsten couldn't really tell him anything until he got the medical power of attorney, but maybe she could at least put his mind at ease concerning Cora's condition.

With a heavy sigh, Brady returned to Cora's room. Her roommate sat in the chair with her eyes fixed on the blaring TV. No wonder Cora wanted to escape. He would, too.

"While you were out asking our pretty nurse for a date, I got ready for bed."

"By yourself?"

"Do you think I'm helpless?"

"Well, no, but I don't want you falling down again."

Cora waved a hand at him. "I have to learn to get around on my own."

"Okay, I guess, and for the record, I wasn't asking anyone for a date." Brady hoped his grandmother wouldn't embarrass him with this date business when Kirsten came to the room.

For the next half hour, Brady answered Cora's battery of questions about what he'd been doing since he'd gotten out of the army. He filled in the gaps between the postcards he'd sent and the infrequent phone calls he'd made to her. Her questions reminded him of his inattentiveness and made him feel more and more guilty that he'd neglected to keep in touch. "Alaska is too beautiful to describe, especially compared to Texas and North Dakota."

"How nice that you could travel and see so many places. That's one thing I wished I could've done, but I never had the money to travel." Cora picked up a book lying next to her Bible. "But I can travel the world by reading a book or listening to you. Do you have photos?"

"A few." Brady pulled his phone from the pocket of his jeans and scrolled through his pictures. "These are some I took when I was in Alaska."

Cora took the phone as Brady showed her how to go through the photos. "Oh, Alaska is a beautiful place. I wish I could go there."

"I wish you could, too."

Wonder painted Cora's wrinkled face as Brady watched her study every picture. He wished he could show her Alaska, but what were the chances his grandmother, with her less-than-good health, could make such a trip? He had a lot of regrets, but he couldn't let regret keep him from moving forward. He couldn't undo the past, but he could try to make the future better. Did that include staying here and putting down roots?

Chaplain Howard used to tell Brady to put it in God's hands. Brady often found that hard to do. He was used to finding his own way and doing his own thing. Trusting God for guidance didn't come easy. In fact, this whole Christian-living thing wasn't easy. He'd been able to survive the cruelty and hardship of war, the physical labor of the oil fields and the treacherous seas of commercial fishing. Humility, putting others first, loving the unlovable—these things required more strength than Brady had on his own.

"Thanks for the tour of Alaska." Cora handed Brady his phone.

"That's only a small part of that big state. I didn't have much time for touring. Too busy working."

As Brady shoved his phone back into his pocket, Kirsten appeared in the doorway. "Ready for that talk?"

Brady nodded, then turned to Cora. "I'll be back in a few minutes. I'm going to talk to Kirsten about the power of attorney you mentioned."

"Good." Cora grinned. "And ask her about that other thing."

Brady shook his head as he hurried toward the door, hoping Cora wouldn't actually say what that other thing was. He wanted to keep this conversation with Kirsten strictly business. He would decide later if he wanted to pursue the social side.

As soon as Brady stepped into the hallway, Kirsten turned and looked at him. Her brown eyes brimmed with curiosity. "What's on your mind?"

Brady couldn't help grinning. Did she know what a loaded question that was? Thoughts floated through his mind. He had to concentrate on Cora, not on the attractive brunette standing in front of him. "I know you can't discuss Cora's specific medical information with me directly, but I was hoping you could give me a general assessment."

"That could be walking a fine line."

"Jen said Cora was making good progress, but I want to know whether her prognosis looks good. When she talks about trying to escape to go to this wedding, I was worried there is more to her condition than the broken hip."

Kirsten opened her mouth, but Brady shook his head and held up a hand. "First, let me tell you Cora asked me to get a medical power of attorney. That worried me because I thought only people who were incapacitated had such things."

"Not necessarily. Your grandmother could use an advocate, not because her health is poor now, but her status could change. And if you have a medical power of attorney, you can talk to her doctor and any of the nurses about Cora's situation." Kirsten nodded. "You should do what she asks."

"I intend to, but I was concerned about her reasons for making the request. How important is it that she attend this wedding?"

"Very important. It's a big event for everyone here. The administrator of this facility is getting married, and your grandmother was a bit of a matchmaker in that love match. I understand her eagerness to witness the nuptials."

"So is there anything I can do besides help her escape?" Brady grinned.

Kirsten narrowed her gaze. "Are you trying to be helpful or trying to be smart?"

Brady contemplated his answer. They'd been having a

congenial conversation, but his last comment had brought out her prickly side again. He should've known the amicable mood wouldn't last, but he hadn't done anything to help. Did the woman ever joke around, or was she always serious? Maybe for now he should be serious, too. "I'm trying to help."

"Good. When you come for a visit, encourage her to take a walk. You could walk with her out to the courtyard out those doors." Kirsten pointed toward the end of the hallway. "Do you plan to stay in the area?"

"I haven't made any definite plans, but I'll be here for a while—at least until Cora goes back to her apartment." Brady wanted to be a help for his grandmother and hoped to find a job here, but there were no guarantees. He couldn't live on his savings forever.

"Good. She needs you right now. And I'll help you every step of the way with your grandmother. We have to be a team. Are you good with that?"

"I am, and I'll be here for her during her recovery." For some strange reason, he wished Kirsten was the one who wanted him to stay. Pure lunacy. He'd just met the woman, and he wasn't even sure he liked her that much. But he liked the idea of being a team with her. Cora's suggestion was eating away at his brain and leaving his thoughts in a knot.

Kirsten glanced at her watch. "Technically, visiting hours are over, but I'll let you stay because it's important to Cora."

"Thanks. I'll say good-night to her, and I'll be out of here." Brady turned to go.

"Wait, Mr. Hewitt. The alarms on the doors are already set, so I'll have to let you out. Stop by the desk before you go."

Brady cringed inwardly when she called him Mr.

Hewitt. She obviously wanted to keep her distance. The seemingly friendly conversation was all business for her, and he should probably keep it that way. So much for Cora's matchmaking abilities in his case.

Chapter Three

The next morning the sunbeams danced between the trees, highlighting the colors of the changing leaves, as Kirsten hurried across the portico of the administration building, with its cobbled pavers and white Georgian columns. But a thundercloud clustered in her mind when she entered the reception area and spied Brady lounging against the desk while he talked with Lovie Trimble, the receptionist, whose greetings never failed to brighten everyone's day. Thinking she could avoid Brady, Kirsten was about to turn around and come in the side entrance when Lovie called to her.

Her plan foiled, Kirsten waved and worked up a smile. She forged ahead while Brady grinned at her. Her opinion hadn't changed. Despite his interest in his grandmother, he came across as cocky, flippant and shallow, doing whatever he could to charm his way through life. She didn't want to talk with him, but she supposed interaction was inevitable while Cora was in the nursing facility.

"Hi, Lovie, Brady. How's everything?"

"Good." Lovie's brown eyes twinkled. "So I see you've met Cora's grandson already."

Kirsten didn't trust the look in Lovie's eyes. She nodded and hoped the older woman didn't try any of her matchmaking plays today. The silver-haired grandmother prided herself on being the first to recognize that Ian and Annie belonged together. Now she considered herself an expert in romance. She was working double time to find a match for the women's ministries director, Melody Hammond. Kirsten hoped Lovie's focus remained on Melody, but Kirsten didn't see Brady as much of a match for Melody, either.

Brady waved a paper in Kirsten's direction. "Got my medical power of attorney."

"So, then you've met Ian?" Kirsten asked.

"Yeah, he got me what I needed." Brady nodded in her direction. "Now you can tell me everything I need to know. How about lunch?"

Kirsten didn't know what to make of his invitation. Was this strictly business or something else? Why had she even asked that question? Of course it was business. He wanted to know about Cora. "I can't today. I'm going to lunch with my dad. In fact, I'm here to meet him."

"He works here?"

"Yes. My dad's Adam Bailey, the director here at The Village of Hope."

An expression Kirsten couldn't define crossed Brady's face. "Ian said I should meet the director of The Village. Will you introduce me?"

Kirsten didn't see how she could refuse Brady's request. "Sure. Come with me, and you can meet him before we go to lunch."

"Thanks." Brady turned back to Lovie. "Good to meet you. I'll be seeing you around."

"Welcome to The Village. You take care of that grandmother of yours. Grandmothers are important people." Lovie patted her silver hair.

"You can count on it." Brady fell into step beside Kirsten. "Is this lunch a special occasion?"

"Not really. We do this a few times a month." What would her father think when she showed up with a guy sporting a dozen tattoos? Probably nothing as long as his daughter didn't want to date the man. Her dad was used to dealing with people who flaunted tattoos, nose rings and the like. He'd learned not to judge people by their outward appearances except when it came to *her* dating choices. Then it was a completely different story.

"Must be nice to be close to your parents."

"Parent." Kirsten stopped in front of a door beside a brass plate engraved with Adam Bailey's name. Before she opened the door, she turned and looked at him. "My mother passed away not quite a year ago."

"I'm sorry. I didn't know." He dropped his gaze. "I shouldn't have assumed."

"That's okay." His statement about being close to parents was odd considering he hadn't cared enough about his grandmother to visit her in years. Cora seemed to dote on him even though she had mentioned parting with Brady on a bad note. Kirsten knew she should be less judgmental, but the bad thoughts about Brady didn't subside. Although she'd lost her mother, she had no idea what it would feel like to lose a mother as a young child and then be abandoned by a father, too.

"How's your dad doing?"

Brady's question surprised Kirsten. Maybe the guy did care about other people. He was hard to figure out. One minute he seemed self-absorbed, the next he was asking about her dad. She shouldn't be afraid to get to know him, but she sensed danger lurking around him. Surely she was overreacting. "I guess as well as can be expected. He doesn't like to talk about it, and I'm not sure whether that's good or bad."

Brady shrugged. "I'm sure he's glad you're around to help him through this."

Another surprising statement. "Yeah, but being nearby gives him too much time to think of ways to run my life."

"That's why you're working here?"

"No. That was my choice, but he wasn't happy when I decided to get my own place." Kirsten put her hand on the doorknob. "Do you suppose his ears are burning since we've been standing out here talking about him?"

Brady gave her a wry smile. "He's probably wondering what's keeping you."

Kirsten glanced at her watch and opened the door. "No. Right on time."

"Is your dad a stickler for being on time?"

"Absolutely, but he's had to cut other people some slack because car trouble has made him late several times in the past few months." Kirsten stepped into her dad's office and spied him standing next to the printer as it spewed forth papers. "Hey, Dad. You ready for lunch?"

Adam looked to the clock on the wall. "Ready."

Kirsten gave her dad a hug. "Dad, I want you to meet Brady Hewitt."

An expression of concern flashed across her dad's features as he extended his hand. "Nice to meet you, Brady."

Her dad's expression made Kirsten wonder whether he was worried that Brady was her new love interest. She'd better put her dad's mind at ease. "Brady is Cora Barton's grandson. You remember Cora, right?"

Adam nodded as the tension in his shoulders appeared to ease. "Your grandmother is a lovely lady. We enjoy having her here at The Village. I understand she's making a good recovery from her broken hip."

"It seems so. I need to give you one of these for your records." Brady handed an envelope to Adam. "This is a copy of the medical power of attorney I have for my grandmother."

Adam took the envelope. "She's smart to have you do this. As our residents age, it's good to have someone to help them with their medical decisions. I'll file this away right now."

Kirsten gave Brady a tentative smile while her father disappeared into a smaller room off his office. Now what? She didn't want to invite Brady to lunch. His presence would remind her of her ill-fated college romance—the one her father had discouraged, and the one she should've known was a wrongheaded choice. Her father had been right about the guy who eventually broke her heart. She'd assumed her father was judging her former boyfriend on his tattoos, earring and long hair, but she realized later that wasn't the case. Her father had seen through the guy's charming facade while she'd been completely oblivious to his deceptions.

Her father had recognized bad character when she hadn't. She'd hated knowing her dad had been right, and she'd been so wrong. Her broken heart had led her to the mission field. The situation had shown her that God could use any circumstance for His purpose. But even after that experience, she had a hard time always seeing God's hand in unfortunate events—like her mother's death or the lost opportunity to adopt three little children. What good had come from that?

"Thanks for the introduction." Brady turned toward the door. "I'll probably see you later when you come on duty."

"Sure." Kirsten breathed an inward sigh of relief as Brady opened the door.

"Brady." Adam stepped back into the room. "Kirsten and I are about to go to lunch. We'd like you to join us."

Speak for yourself, Dad. Kirsten bit back the words. She looked at Brady to gauge his reaction to the invitation.

Brady smiled, then looked at her as if he was seeking her approval. "Sure. Thanks for inviting me."

Brady's expression didn't go along with his brash attitude. Maybe she'd imagined the look. She didn't want him to go to lunch with them. With her dad there, she wouldn't be able to tell Brady anything about Cora. So why did he want to go? Shouldn't he be having lunch with Cora?

Kirsten tried not to analyze the situation further as she followed her dad and Brady to her dad's car. She needed to develop a better attitude. Today's lunch with her dad and Brady would test her ability to reach that goal.

The white iridescent vase full of pink roses and white calla lilies shimmered like a neon sign as it sat on the counter at the nurses' station. The bouquet seemed to whisper, *I'm really a nice guy. You just need to get to know me.* Kirsten tried to purge the imagined message from her thoughts.

"I'd say Brady's trying to impress you." Jen grinned.

"He's just thanking me for introducing him to my dad." Kirsten wondered whether Brady had asked her dad about her favorite flowers. Otherwise, how would he have known?

Jen gave Kirsten a dubious look. "There's more to those flowers than a thank-you."

Kirsten shook her head. "You have no idea what happened yesterday."

"I'm all ears. Give me the scoop." Jen settled back in her chair.

"When I introduced Brady to my dad, he invited the guy to lunch." Kirsten shrugged and held up her hands in a gesture of helplessness. "That's the last thing I wanted, but it gets worse."

"How does worse translate to this beautiful bouquet?" Jen gestured toward the flowers.

"First, we were talking about the wedding. Then Brady says he needs to get a suit, so Dad invites him over to check out one of his suits."

"So your dad lent the guy a suit. What's so bad about that?"

"Nothing if it had stopped there." Kirsten released a loud sigh. "When I stopped by Dad's office before I came to work, he informed me that Brady is going to rent a room from him—not just any room, but my old room."

"You didn't want it, so what's the problem?"

Kirsten shook her head. "I don't know. It seems weird to have this guy living in my old room."

"Did you ever think your dad might be lonely, and having someone else in the house is a real plus? It's probably a win-win for both of them. Your dad doesn't have to come home to an empty house, and Brady has an inexpensive place to live while he looks for a job."

"I suppose you're right."

While Kirsten checked patient records on the computer screen, she wondered what Brady might be hiding. Why was his job experience something he'd had to think about at lunch? Had he been involved with something illegal? Those tattoos could mean he'd been in some kind of gang or something. Maybe she'd been reading too many suspense books lately.

"I'm not quite sure why you have this hostility toward the guy."

"It's not animus. It's caution." Kirsten looked up.

"And why do you have to be cautious of a man who sends flowers?"

"You've answered your own question. Why did he send flowers?"

"To say thank-you. That's what you said."

"I was only trying to find an explanation, but he may have some ulterior motive." Kirsten frowned. "What do we really know about him other than his relationship to Cora?"

"He's good-looking." Jen grinned.

Kirsten swatted at Jen. "Be serious. I'm worried about my dad inviting a stranger to share the house."

"Don't you remember the scripture from *Hebrews* that says if you practice hospitality you might unknowingly entertain angels?"

Kirsten didn't want to think about the scripture reference. "He's the only family Cora has left. He should've let her know where he was."

"Fair enough, but I'd say he's trying to make up for it now. Give him a chance to prove himself. You could still ask him to be your date for the wedding and get to know him better."

"And why would I want to do that?"

Jen raised her eyebrows. "Because he's good-looking?"

"Give up. I'm not interested." Kirsten's thoughts about Brady battled back and forth. One minute she was ready to cut him some slack because he had a legitimate reason for not answering his phone messages, but the next minute she couldn't forget Cora's distress when they couldn't reach him.

He still had years of neglect to answer for. If you loved

someone, how could you ignore them for months at a time, especially a grandmother who'd raised you? Kirsten's judgmental attitude didn't die easily when it came to Brady.

Jen shook her head. "You know what they say. Never give up."

"Please. He's only twenty-nine. I'm five years older than he is."

"Is that a problem?"

"I don't think it's a problem." A male voice sounded from around the corner an instant before Brady appeared.

Kirsten's heart plummeted into her stomach as she quickly lowered her gaze. Her face flaming hot, she didn't dare to look up. How much of the conversation had Brady heard? He must have heard enough to know they'd been talking about him. She wanted to crawl under the desk. What could she possibly say? Now he would surely have the wrong impression. Deciding not to respond to his comment, she shot a dagger-filled look in Jen's direction, then finally found the courage to smile at Brady. "Thanks for the flowers. They're lovely. My favorites."

Brady grinned. "Your dad said you'd like them. Did Cora like hers?"

"I haven't been down to her room since I came on duty. If they're as beautiful as these, I'm sure she did." Kirsten let this information filter through her mind. So Brady liked sending flowers. There was nothing special about her bouquet. Why did that disappoint her?

"I've been job hunting most of the day."

"Any success?" Kirsten hoped her question would permanently steer the conversation away from her comment about his age.

Brady nodded. "I have a few leads. The job counselor

here was very helpful. I'm glad your dad suggested I talk to her."

"My dad tells me you're renting a room from him."

"Yeah. It's a real help while I'm trying to find a job."

"I'm glad he was able to help you."

"Me, too." Brady winked at her. "And for the record. I like older women. Underneath your prickly exterior, I'm sure there's a heart of gold. And I intend to find it."

Kirsten stared after Brady as he sauntered down the hallway without a backward glance. How had he managed to insult and compliment her all in one statement? How could such an insolent man make her heart flutter?

Jen swiveled her chair until she was facing Kirsten, then laughed out loud. "This is going to be fun to watch."

"There isn't going to be anything to watch." Kirsten was determined not to let him get under her skin or into her heart.

Jen laughed again. "I wouldn't count on that. I'm pretty sure Brady Hewitt doesn't lose when he sets his mind to something."

"Count on this. Brady Hewitt has met his match."

"You might be right." Jen smirked. "You realize what you just said, right?"

Kirsten shook her head. "Don't misinterpret my meaning."

"The way I see it, there is no misinterpreting the sparks flying around here when you two are together."

"Don't you have work to do?" Kirsten narrowed her gaze.

Jen glanced at her watch. "Yeah, I'm off to deliver meds."

As Jen pushed her cart down the hallway, Kirsten rubbed her temples with her fingertips. Brady Hewitt was one big headache. At least he let you know where you stood with him.

Was she huffy, or was it only with him? He seemed to bring out her judgmental side, and that wasn't a good way to be. Had God sent Brady into her life to help her see the need to change her attitude?

Do you ever think these things have happened because God has another plan for your life? Jen's question floated through Kirsten's mind.

Kirsten didn't want her plans to be different, but the future didn't lie in her hands. She had no control over the Brazilian government's decision on her visa or Brady's presence at The Village. She would have to make the best of whatever came her way—like it or not.

"How's the physical therapy going?" Kirsten patted Cora's shoulder.

A weak smile curved Cora's lips, and her shoulders sagged. "It's grueling. I'm worn out when they're done with me."

"I know. But think of the reward. You get to go to the wedding."

Cora nodded. "That's the only thing that keeps me going besides having Brady here. Thank you for your efforts to contact him. Just seeing him brightens my day."

"I'm glad I could help." Kirsten had to admit Brady's presence had given Cora a lift. Kirsten hadn't expected that.

"I don't know what I'd do without this place. Y'all have given me a lot of hope."

"That's what we're here for. After all, this is The Village of Hope. Hope is the most important thing we have around here." Kirsten looked at Cora with sympathy.

Nodding, Cora sighed. "Hope in the Lord Jesus."

"That's who we depend on for sure."

"I know. Say some prayers for my strength."

"I will, and you can concentrate on your physical therapy so you can regain your strength and can get out of that wheelchair."

"And return to my apartment."

"Yes. The harder you work, the faster you get better." Kirsten headed for the door but turned before she left the room. "Remember. You don't get over a broken hip overnight."

Cora wagged a gnarled finger at Kirsten. "Yes, but I'm not the most patient person. I like things to happen right now."

"You don't have many days left until the wedding." Kirsten put a hand to her cart. "I think you'll be ready."

"I'd better be. Brady is so good to take me for walks." Cora grinned. "We're going to walk all the way to the cafeteria tonight for supper. I'm so excited to eat with Ruby and Liz."

"That's super news." Kirsten couldn't get over how attentive Brady was to his grandmother. The man appeared to be doing everything he could to help the woman who'd done her best to give him a good life. "Have fun with Ruby and Liz."

"Well, if it isn't my favorite grandmother and my favorite nurse."

Kirsten turned to find Brady lounging in the doorway. Her heart did a little flip-flop. Why did this exasperating man make her react that way? It had to be his unexpected entrance. But she shouldn't be surprised he was here. He'd shown up at this time every day for the past week, and she tried to convince herself that she didn't look forward to his visit.

"Well, if it isn't the favorite grandson." Kirsten pressed her lips together in order not to smile.

"I'm glad you recognize that." Brady walked across

the room and gave Cora a kiss on her cheek. "Hey, Gram, how's it going today?"

"Good. I'm looking forward to dinner with Ruby and Liz."

"Have a good evening, you two. I have to deliver the rest of these meds." Kirsten scurried out the door as the thought of Brady giving her a kiss the way he had Cora flitted through her mind. Why had that happened? Jen's constant chatter about how Brady timed his visits so he'd see Kirsten made her think crazy things.

After Kirsten finished delivering medications to the patients on her wing of the nursing home, she returned to the nurses' station. She plopped onto the nearby chair with a sigh and stared at the computer screen. The week-old vase of flowers, still surprisingly fresh, taunted her from the ledge above her. Another reminder of Brady. Thankfully, Jen was off helping a patient, so Kirsten didn't have to listen to any more of the other nurse's teasing.

Pushing thoughts of Brady from her mind, Kirsten concentrated on the patient records as she input the information into the computer. She missed the day-to-day hands-on work with patients in Brazil, especially the little children. She enjoyed helping the elderly patients here but didn't relish the extensive amount of record keeping.

"Kirsten."

The sound of a familiar male voice made Kirsten jump. She jerked her head upward to find Brady standing on the other side of the counter. She put a hand over her heart. "You scared me. You certainly are quiet when you walk."

"All the better to surprise you. You were obviously lost in your work." He gave her that lazy grin. "Do you have a minute to talk?"

"Sure." Kirsten wondered what he wanted to talk about that he couldn't have mentioned while she was in Cora's room.

"Good." He leaned on the counter next to the bouquet. He glanced at them. "Flowers still look good. Nice to know where to get good ones."

"How's my dad working out as a roommate?"

"Good."

Staring at Brady, Kirsten wondered how she was going to get rid of him without being impolite. She didn't want him hanging around here when Jen got back. That would mean listening to her supposition that Brady was out to impress Kirsten. "Was there something special you wanted to talk about?"

"Yeah, there is." He rubbed the back of his neck and said nothing else.

Why was he hesitant? His uncertainty was completely out of character. She leaned forward. "And that would be?"

"I want to buy something for Cora, and I need your help."

"Why my help?"

"Because you're a woman."

"And you need a woman's advice?" Was he reluctant to ask a woman for help?

"Yeah."

"Okay, I'm willing to assist you. What do I have to do?" Had she said that? No telling what he might ask.

"Go shopping with me tomorrow."

Kirsten forced herself not to show she was the least bit put out by his ploy. He didn't need acting lessons. He had the apprehension charade down. She had no one to blame but herself for walking right into his act. "And what will we be shopping for?"

"A dress for Cora to wear to the wedding."

"And you can't do that without my help?"

"No. Besides, your dad suggested I ask you when I mentioned buying the dress."

"Okay." Kirsten tried not to frown. What was her dad up to? Was he trying to push them together? "What time?"

"You name it."

"Meet me at the reception desk at half past nine. That way we can be at the mall by the time the stores open."

"Thanks. I look forward to it." Brady turned and sauntered back down the hall.

Kirsten couldn't help watching him walk away. *Now there's a fine-looking man.* Jen's words echoed through Kirsten's mind. He was growing on her. Lately she hadn't even noticed his tattoos. Was she inviting trouble by letting down her guard with regard to Brady and his considerable charm? She didn't dare mention it to Jen, or she would never give Kirsten a minute of peace about it. She could purge these thoughts from her mind on her own. She knew from experience that charming men only brought heartache.

Chapter Four

Gray skies greeted Brady as he headed to The Village, but he wouldn't let them dampen his good mood. He parked his pickup near the administration building. When he entered the reception area, Kirsten was talking with Lovie. Kirsten turned in his direction as he drew closer. When she smiled, his heart did a little tap dance. What did his reaction say about how he was feeling about her?

He was pretty sure Kirsten's negative opinion of him was changing, and he was glad for it. But did that mean he could convince her to go out with him?

"Hey, Lovie, Kirsten. How are you ladies doing this morning?"

"Good," they both answered.

Kirsten stepped away from the reception desk. "Ready to go? I'll drive."

Brady nodded, then waved to Lovie and followed Kirsten out a side door. "I checked the size of the dress hanging in her closet while she was napping yesterday."

"What is it?"

"Eight P. Whatever that means."

"It means eight petite. That sounds about right." Kirsten opened her car door.

"So you're taking me to the closest mall?" Brady adjusted the passenger seat as he settled in the car and buckled his seat belt.

"That's right. We should be able to find something there."

Brady watched in silence as Kirsten maneuvered through the traffic until they came to a traffic light. "When I was a kid, Cora lived about a mile from here. You know, this road had barely anything on it then. Now it's lined with big-box stores, strip malls and fast-food restaurants. Urban sprawl, with its traffic jams and housing developments, has created chaos and taken over this once-quiet road."

"I take it you're not a fan of big-city living." Kirsten looked straight ahead as the light changed and she drove through the intersection.

Brady shook his head. "After living in North Dakota and west Texas, where you can see forever, all these trees make me feel closed in—claustrophobic."

"So it's not only the urban sprawl, but the landscape, too."

"Yeah."

"Does that mean you plan to leave after Cora gets better?"

"I don't know what it means. A lot depends on my job search."

"How's that going?"

"Too early to tell. I've filled out a lot of applications and had one interview. I don't know anything beyond that."

"Has Cora told you how much she'd like you to stay?"

Brady couldn't decipher the meaning of Kirsten's question. Was she trying to tell him he should stay no matter what? "I don't believe she's thought about much beyond that wedding."

"She's thinking beyond the wedding. She wants to get back to her apartment."

"And I'm going to see that she gets there. I want to be the person she can count on when she needs help." Brady wished he'd been more attentive to Cora in the past. He was going to make up for that now. He had to find a job. He hated the thought of living here permanently, but if he was going to be there for Cora, that's what had to be done.

"Then I guess that means you intend to stay."

"I still have to find a job."

"What kind of job are you looking for?" Kirsten glanced at him as she turned into the mall entrance.

Brady wasn't sure. What would Kirsten say if she knew he had medical experience? He'd only mentioned his work on oil rigs and a fishing boat when they'd had lunch with her dad. In the army he'd been a medic, and he'd been good at it. But he'd discovered after getting out that despite his experience, the only jobs he qualified for in the medical field paid little over minimum wage. He couldn't survive on that long-term, so he'd found employment wherever he could. Those jobs had paid well, and he had a healthy savings account. "Something that pays a decent wage."

"Have you considered taking a temporary job until you find something better?"

"Not until it becomes clear that I can't find a good-paying job."

Kirsten found a parking spot near an entrance. "We'll start with the nearest department store, and if we don't find anything there, we'll try the specialty shops, then move on to other places."

Nodding, Brady noted how she'd abruptly changed

the subject. Did she think he was finding excuses not to stay? "You're in charge."

They entered the mall through one of the anchor department stores. When they reached the area for petite women's clothing, Kirsten headed straight for the dresses. "How fancy do you want the dress?"

Brady stared at her. What did he know about women's dresses? For men, a suit of some kind always sufficed. "What do you think?"

"Do you want bling on the dress?"

"What?"

"Bling. Like sparkly stuff."

Brady shrugged. "If that's what you think."

Kirsten forged ahead of him. He followed, thankful that he wasn't doing this on his own. She rummaged through the racks and scooped up a half-dozen dresses and hung them over her arm.

"Would you like me to hold them?"

She glanced at him. "Sure, and I'll look at this last rack."

Brady held the hangers and studied the dresses. They were nice, but he didn't think any of them suited Cora. He walked over to where Kirsten was looking. "Have you run across anything in green?"

Kirsten frowned. "Not many. Black or neutral colors seem to be the going style."

"But with her white hair doesn't she need some color?"

Kirsten stopped and looked at him as if he had two heads. "Are you sure you need help? You seem to know what you want."

"Yes, I need your help." He gave her a wry smile. "How would I have found the special-occasion dresses section without you?"

Kirsten crossed her arms. "I think you could have managed."

"But it wouldn't be nearly as fun doing this alone. I'm enjoying your company." Smiling wryly, Brady held up one of the dresses. "I like this one with the lace and sparkly stuff here, but I'd like it in a bright color."

"I'll put those back on the rack, and we'll move on to another store." Sighing, Kirsten held out a hand for the dresses.

As Brady handed them to her, their fingers brushed. There was no mistaking the look that crossed her face. The touch had the same effect on her as it had on him. The attraction he was feeling wasn't all one-sided. That was a good sign.

She scurried away. Was she running away from their obvious attraction to each other? He closed the gap between them. "You're in a hurry."

"Have to be. We have a lot of ground to cover."

Brady stared after her again. Despite her apparent attraction to him, she still seemed uncomfortable around him. Could he figure out why? Maybe her dad could shed some light on his daughter, but asking her father might not be a good idea.

Why did he even care, anyway? He was here for Cora, not to make friends with a prickly nurse.

But he knew why. He wanted to be liked. It was just how he'd always been.

He shook those thoughts away as Kirsten dragged him from store to store. They continued to find nothing. Why did women like to shop? He was developing a full-blown headache. What if the dress he'd envisioned didn't exist?

As they left a specialty shop without success, Kirsten turned to him. "We have one more department store to check."

"What if we don't find anything there?"

"We will."

"Okay. I hope you're right." Brady traipsed into the department store, his hopes about as low as they could get. Still, he wanted to see the surprise and delight on Cora's face when he presented her with the dress. Was that going to happen? Maybe buying a dress for Cora had been a thoughtful idea, but not very practical.

Kirsten did her usual search through the racks, grabbing a dress here and there as she went. At least this time she carried a rainbow of colors on her arm. Brady trailed after her. "Need help?"

She shook her head as she forged ahead. Since she'd handed him the dresses in the first store and their fingers had touched, she'd avoided giving him anything to hold.

"Give me your opinion." She held up the first dress.

"It's okay, but I think it's a little long. I wouldn't want Cora to trip on it. She has her walker to deal with."

"Okay." Kirsten laid the dress aside on the top of the nearby rack and held up the next one.

Brady shook his head. "It's green, but it's kind of a washed-out green."

Kirsten showed him another dress. "I like the cranberry color."

"Yeah, it's bright." Brady shrugged. "But it doesn't have any *bling*, as you say."

Kirsten chuckled. "You may have to compromise. Something tells me the perfect dress you have in mind doesn't exist. What about this?"

"Too low cut."

"This one?"

"Too short."

Kirsten smiled. "Making sure she doesn't show too much skin?"

"Yeah. I wouldn't want her to accuse me of dressing her like a floozy, as she would say." Brady smiled, thinking maybe he'd found Kirsten's less serious side. She'd actually joked about something.

"Did Cora warn you about them?"

Brady let the question settle in his mind. Did he dare admit the existence of that kind of woman in his life? Those days were behind him. What good would come from bringing up his past? "Let's finish looking at the dresses."

"Sure." Kirsten offered up another dress.

The dress practically danced on the hanger as Brady stared at it. This was it. He could see Cora wearing this dress. "What color would you say this is?"

Cocking her head, Kirsten studied the dress as she held it out in front of her. "I'd say it's multiple shades of purple." She ran her hand across the shimmery material. "And the beading at the neckline makes a nice accent. You like this one?"

"Yeah. What do you think?"

"It doesn't matter what I think. You're the one who has to like it."

"Actually, Cora's the one who has to like it. What if she doesn't?" Brady furrowed his brow. "Guess I better rethink the idea of surprising her on the day of the wedding."

"I think she'll love it. It's a beautiful dress. And it'll be a surprise no matter when you give it to her."

"Okay." After locating the checkout, Brady handed the dress to the sales associate.

As she scanned the bar code and the price came up on the little screen, he realized he hadn't looked at the price. When had women's dresses become so pricey? Not that he'd ever bought a woman's dress before, but he'd never paid that much for a suit. And thankfully he didn't have to buy one this time since Kirsten's dad had loaned him one. Still, his grandmother was worth every penny he'd spent on her. After he paid, the clerk handed him the dress in a fancy garment bag. A dress that expensive deserved a special bag. He hooked the hanger over a couple of fingers and slung it over his back as they headed for the mall exit. "That was a lot of work. Thanks for your help."

"You're welcome." Kirsten smiled. "I kind of enjoyed it after all."

"So you're admitting that I'm a fun guy?" Brady returned her smile, thinking he'd been wrong about Kirsten. She had a serious job. She took things seriously and didn't always like to joke as he did, but she knew how to look on the positive side of things. He hoped that boded well for him in his quest to win her over.

"I wouldn't go that far." She gazed at him, trying to look serious, but another smile escaped.

"You can't fool me. I saw that smile. You really like me."

"You're growing on me."

"Enough to go out to lunch with me?"

She didn't say anything as she unlocked the car doors.

"At least to say thanks for helping me? No pressure. No expectations." He grinned.

Kirsten looked at him as they got into the car. "Do you always grin like that?"

Brady buckled his seat belt. "You can blame the grin on Cora. She always said, 'Keep smiling. It makes people wonder what you've been up to.'"

"That sounds like something she'd say." Kirsten started the car.

"Where'd you like to have lunch?"

Kirsten pulled onto the main road. "Do you have a place where you'd like to go?"

"Probably all the places I used to know aren't around anymore."

"Name one."

"McGurdy's Pizza." Brady gave her a sideways glance. "Do you know the place?"

"Absolutely." Kirsten laughed.

"What's so funny?"

"It's Annie and Ian's favorite place, too."

While Kirsten drove to the pizza place, Brady took in the sights of the suburban sprawl he detested. Could he live here again? He could, but did he want to? He cast a surreptitious look in Kirsten's direction. Could staying here include this pretty woman next to him? This morning had been fun, and he'd seen a different side of her. She didn't hesitate to speak her mind, and he never had to guess where he stood with her. He liked that. He liked a whole lot of things about her, but did she like enough things about him to give him a chance? Or was she out of his league?

Cars of every variety filled McGurdy's parking lot. Wondering what this lunch with Brady would bring, Kirsten managed to find a place to park when someone left with a carryout order. Her feelings about Brady had become quite tangled, ranging from exasperation to fascination. She wanted to untangle them. Would this time together help?

"The place is busy today." Kirsten turned off the engine and opened the door.

Brady hopped out of the car. "Best pizza on this side of Atlanta draws a crowd."

Thankfully, within minutes they were able to find

seats at a booth with a dark wooden plank table located next to a window. The noontime sun beamed in the window and made the table gleam. Menus sat in a rack against the windowsill. Brady grabbed one and gave it to Kirsten.

"Thanks. When was the last time you were here?" Kirsten asked.

"High school." Brady glanced around the place. "It looks pretty much the same. Did you go to high school around here?"

Kirsten shook her head. Was Brady trying to talk about her high school years rather than his because he had unpleasant memories of that time? "We lived in Ohio when I was in high school. Can't you tell that I don't have a Southern accent?"

"You might have moved here when you were in high school." Brady shrugged. "Besides, I've been around so many accents in the past ten years that I hardly notice them."

"Should we order veggie pizza?"

"Now how did I know you'd want to order one of those?" Brady grimaced. "Mind if I add some sausage?"

"Go ahead. Not a fan of veggies?"

"I'd rather eat a steak than a salad."

The waitress appeared and took their order and returned shortly with their drinks. After she left, Kirsten shook her head and laughed halfheartedly. "When it comes to vegetables, you sound like my dad. I was always trying to push the vegetables and fruit while I lived with him."

"He must've taken your advice. He served me a fruit salad the other night when he cooked our meal."

"He did?" Kirsten shook her head. "I can hardly believe it. I'm discovering all kinds of things about my dad. He rarely cooked when I lived there."

"Maybe it's because you did the cooking, and since you've left, he has to fend for himself."

Kirsten nodded. "I started when I came home from Brazil because my mom was so ill. I wanted to help out."

"Your dad said she died from breast cancer."

Kirsten swallowed a lump in her throat. "She was diagnosed with breast cancer before I went to the mission field. She had all the treatments and was cancer-free for ten years, which is usually a good sign. But it came back, and despite the treatments the second time around, she didn't survive. It was really hard on my dad and me."

"I can relate." Brady hung his head for a moment, then glanced up. "It was hard on my dad and me, too, when my mom died in that car accident. Only my dad, unlike yours, couldn't come to grips with his grief. He kind of gave up on life. My dad lost his job and became a drifter. That's why I went to live with Cora. She saved me from winding up in foster care."

"I'm so sorry about your mom and what happened with your dad. You're so fortunate to have your grandmother. She's a wonderful lady."

"Thanks." Brady nodded. "I wasn't always thankful. I was angry and gave her a hard time."

"She told me about the time you took apart your motorcycle in her living room."

Brady shook his head. "Yeah, not one of my finer moments. We had a big falling-out over that. So I dropped out of high school and went in search of my dad."

"Did you find him?"

"Yeah, I found him living on the streets. I did that for a while with him, but I didn't want that kind of life. So I got my GED and joined the army." Brady grimaced.

"After that I lost track of him. I did talk to my uncle, my dad's only brother, when I got out of the service. He said my dad was in and out of mental-health facilities and continued to drift. They even lost track of him. So I have no idea where he is or how he's doing."

Kirsten wasn't sure what to say. What a sad thing for Brady. "Do you ever think about trying to find him again?"

Brady shook his head. "I've come to the conclusion he doesn't care about any of his family and doesn't want to be found. He might not even be alive. I pray for him."

"I'll pray for him, too."

"Thanks."

Before Kirsten could comment, the waitress appeared with their pizza. The young woman flirted with Brady as she brought extra napkins and refilled their drinks. Kirsten tried not to be annoyed.

"Do the waitresses always flirt with you?"

He gave her that familiar grin. "Only the good-looking ones."

"I'm sorry I asked." Kirsten chuckled. "We should give thanks for the food. Would you like to pray?"

He stared at her, those golden-brown eyes filled with uncertainty. He bowed his head. "Lord, thanks for the successful shopping and this food. Amen."

Brady grabbed a slice of pizza and took a big bite.

"As good as you remembered?"

Brady swallowed. "Better."

"It's probably the veggies!" Kirsten laughed.

"You could be right."

They ate for several minutes in companionable silence. Kirsten's mind buzzed with thoughts of the morning's activity, which had been a lot of fun. In the past few minutes she'd learned a great deal about Brady. He'd suffered a lot of tragedy, but he'd managed to bounce back. They shared being only children who'd lost a mother. Was his cavalier attitude an attempt not to dwell on the bad things he'd experienced? He said he prayed for his dad, and Brady had given thanks for their meal. Did that mean he had faith in God, or was it just an expression?

Brady took a big gulp of his drink, then looked at her. "Your dad told me that The Village has a fall festival for a big fund-raiser in a few weeks. I said I'd like to help, and he asked me if I'd work at the food booth."

"Great. I'm in charge of that booth, and we can use all the help we can get." Kirsten tried to put on a happy face. She didn't understand why her dad had nearly adopted Brady. The next thing she knew her dad would be campaigning for Brady to take her to the wedding. Thankfully, she didn't have to worry about that because he already had a date. Cora.

"What will my job entail?" Brady was grinning as if he knew her consternation.

Obviously she was very transparent. Did he know how confused she was about him? She wasn't going to let him see her squirm. "We can always use another burger flipper."

"And jack-of-all-trades. I can swing a mean hammer, too, if you need that kind of help."

"We can use whatever help we can get. Just don't hammer the burgers."

Brady leaned his head back and laughed. When he returned his gaze to hers, he shook his head. "I guess you have a sense of humor after all."

Kirsten's midsection dipped and swirled. She took a deep breath, not sure if her reaction was exasperation or satisfaction that she'd made him laugh. "Of course, I do. You'll see how humorous I can be when we're working together."

"I'm looking forward to it."

"The fall festival is always a good time and it's for a great cause."

"And I want to be a part of that." Brady nodded. "I've been thinking. When we get back, I'm going to give Cora the dress. That way if she doesn't like it, I'll still have time to look for something else."

Kirsten set down her slice of pizza, realizing how much this gift for his grandmother meant to Brady. "It's up to you."

"Would you like to join me? After all, you did help me find it."

"I'd like that." With a smile, Kirsten looked over at Brady. His charm was drawing her in. Was she a pushover for charming men? Men like Lance, who had only pretended he cared? She'd practically forgotten about Brady's scruffy look and tattoos, but his sometimes flippant attitude still gave her pause. She had to remember that it was the heart that counted—and Brady's heart cared about his grandmother.

Kirsten wasn't sure she could trust her own judgment when it came to men. Lance hadn't been the only man who'd turned on her. Her worst heartache had come when she'd been training for the mission field. She'd fallen in love with Will Peterson while they were in preparation to serve, but as soon as he found out she couldn't have children, he'd backed away.

Her work in Brazil had filled the void of failed romances. She found her happiness in service to the needy. But now her work didn't consume her every thought and movement. She had to admit she was vulnerable to Brady's charm. She had to be wary, or she would fall into the same pattern—letting herself care about a man who would only break her heart.

After finishing two slices of pizza, Kirsten leaned back with a sigh. "That was good."

"I'll get a box for the leftovers, and then we'll head over to see Cora."

For the first few minutes of the drive back to The Village, neither of them spoke. Kirsten wondered why Brady hadn't asked about Cora's medical issues now that he had medical power of attorney. Maybe he was satisfied with what he knew, or maybe he had asked one of the other nurses. She wanted to ask, but it wasn't her place to do so.

"What's with the fountain on campus having colored water and balloons from time to time?" Brady's question shook her from her thoughts.

She turned to him. "Someone sponsored the fountain for a celebration."

"Sponsored the fountain?"

"Yeah. Like paid to have the balloons and colored water. It could be a birthday, anniversary or anything a person wanted to celebrate. If you sponsor the fountain, you can request the decorations we have listed on The Village website."

He nodded thoughtfully. "So if I wanted to do this for Cora's birthday, I could?"

"Absolutely. When is her birthday?"

"Not till February, but it's something to plan for."

Kirsten couldn't help notice the way Brady stared off into space as she stopped at a traffic light. Did she dare ask what he was thinking? "You have some thoughts about it."

"I was thinking she'd like green." He shrugged. "I remember the fountain from the time I came for soccer camp during my middle school years when this place was Upton College. What happened to the college?"

The traffic light turned green, and Kirsten drove ahead. "The enrollment went way down, and it fell into financial trouble. When they closed the college, a group of folks had a vision to create a place to help the less fortunate. Didn't my dad tell you anything about The Village?"

Brady shrugged. "We haven't talked much about The Village, at least not in any detail. Besides, I didn't want to intrude on your dad's time or space."

Kirsten hadn't asked her dad about his new situation— maybe because her initial reaction to the development had been negative. She hadn't wanted to seem too nosy or too interested in Brady. "So you're saying you talk very little to each other?"

"We speak, but mostly about sports. Your dad doesn't say much otherwise. And I'm not much of a conversationalist myself."

Only when he wanted to charm his way into or around something. Then Brady was as glib as they came. "You could've fooled me."

She glanced his way and once again he gave her that lazy smile that brought butterflies to her stomach. "I always like talking to pretty women," he said easily.

"I should've guessed."

Brady chuckled. "You should have. I like talking to you."

Kirsten refused to take his statement personally, deciding to ignore it. "Has anyone taken you on a tour of The Village campus?" she asked as the guard waved them through the gate at the entrance to The Village.

"Are you volunteering?" The hint of a smile resided at the corners of his mouth.

Was she? She didn't answer immediately as she parked the car in the parking lot nearest to the nursing home. Today had already yielded information about Brady that made her see him in a different light. Would showing him around help her know him better, or would spending more time with him contribute to the attraction she had no business harboring. She had plans to return to Brazil and getting involved with anyone was not an option. "We'll see. If I can't, I'm sure my dad would be happy to show you the place. He's eager to show people the work we do here."

Brady grabbed Cora's dress and exited the car, looking at Kirsten over the top as she locked the door. "But being with you would be so much more fun."

"Sometimes we have to put aside fun for other duties."

"Sometimes we have to have fun. But since I can't interest you in fun, as you put it, could you explain why you have such tight security here? What's going on that requires gates and guards and check-ins wherever you go on campus?"

Kirsten motioned toward the quad. "The main reason for the security is our women's shelter on the far side of the quad. Some of the women living there have fled abusive and sometimes life-threatening relationships. No place is completely secure, but we try our best to keep them safe."

"That makes sense." Brady nodded. "I had my reservations about Cora living at The Village, but she seems to like it."

Kirsten wondered when he had ever thought about his grandmother when he'd been so far away for so many years. The negative thought slipped into her mind. She shook it away. Positive thoughts should dictate their discussion. "We love having her."

"I wish I'd been a better grandson. I should've kept in touch and visited more."

Kirsten studied his expression and tried to figure out whether he was saying this because he really meant it or because he was trying to get on her good side. There it was again—another judgmental thought, the sin she struggled with the most. *Lord, please take away my judgmental attitude.*

"Cora's glad you're here now."

"Is she going to be okay?"

"As long as she keeps progressing with her physical therapy. When she broke her hip, the docs ran tests to make sure she hadn't had another stroke."

"Did she?"

"No. Other than the broken hip, she has no other problems. She's doing quite well. That's the most important part."

"Is there anything else I need to know?"

"Not right now, but you can make an inquiry about her status anytime. Talk to Cora about what you know." So he was finally asking about Cora. What had taken him so long after he'd gotten the medical power of attorney? Kirsten forced herself to keep a positive tone. "You've been a big help to her since you've arrived."

"I hope so." Brady opened the door for Kirsten then strode down the hallway. "You've been a big help to your dad, too. That's one thing he did say to me."

"I'm glad to hear that. My dad didn't seem too happy when I moved out, but I wanted him to be prepared for the day I go back to Brazil."

"You're going back?"

Kirsten sighed. "Hopefully. I miss my work with the children there. They have so little, and we have so much to give. But I'm having difficulty getting a new missionary visa."

"Cora will be disappointed if you return to Brazil."

Was Brady disappointed, too? The question flitted across Kirsten's mind, but she dismissed it immediately. It didn't matter. She planned to leave. "She won't need me after she moves back to her apartment, but she'll always need you."

Brady forged ahead without making a response. When they arrived at Cora's room, she was sitting in her chair, reading. Kirsten hung back. Although she wanted to be there, she didn't want to intrude on this time Brady had with his grandmother.

He crossed the room, the garment bag behind his back. "Hey, Gram. How are you today?"

Looking up, Cora laid her book aside. "Brady, I'm so glad you're here. I have good news."

"What's that?"

"The physical therapist gave the go-ahead for me to attend the wedding and the reception!"

"I knew you could do it." Brady still held the bag behind his back. "I was certain you would get to go. So I have a little surprise for you."

Cora's wrinkled face lit up. "You do? What?"

Brady held the bag out in front of him. "A new dress for you to wear."

"Oh, my." Cora reached for her walker and pushed herself to a standing position. "Let me see it."

"I hope you like it." Brady turned to Kirsten. "Will you hold this while I unzip it?"

"Sure." Kirsten took the bag, careful not to make contact. "Hi, Cora. You're going to love this."

Brady pulled out the dress and held it up for Cora to see. The wonder and love on the faces of grandmother and grandson made Kirsten's heart melt. Her eyes got a little misty as Cora ran a hand over the shimmery material.

"What do you think, Gram?"

Cora put her other hand over her heart and looked at Brady with tears welling in her eyes. "It's beautiful. How did you know I love lavender?"

Brady grinned. "Good guess."

Cora hugged Brady, then looked over at Kirsten. "Did you help in this venture?"

"I guided him through the mall, but he picked out the dress." Kirsten glanced at Brady. "Let's have her model it for us."

While Brady waited in the hallway, Kirsten helped Cora put on her new dress, zipping up the back. "You look fabulous. How about walking out to the hallway for a little fashion show?"

Cora pushed her walker into the hallway where a group of nurses and aides had gathered around Brady. Cora tried to frown, but the smile in her eyes gave her away. "Did you bring these people here to look at me?"

"I did, and you look fabulous." Brady gave her a hug as everyone applauded. "Other than the bride and groom, we'll be the best-dressed couple there."

"I know my grandson will be the most handsome man there." Cora smoothed the skirt as she looked at Kirsten. "He's a treasure."

Kirsten nodded, not wanting to give a hint that she might have doubts about Cora's statement. Was Brady a treasure? Maybe a diamond in the rough. But after today, Kirsten would have a harder time disagreeing with Cora. He was slowly inching his way into her heart. Should she let it happen?

Chapter Five

As Annie walked down the aisle of the crowded Chapel Church on The Village of Hope campus, Kirsten didn't doubt that, given a chance, true love could triumph over the most difficult circumstances. Ian and Annie's story was one of overcoming substance abuse and betrayal. With God's help, they'd found each other again. Everything from Annie's perfect dress to the sparkle in Ian's eyes as he watched his bride come to him made Kirsten wish she could find such happiness. Would she ever find a man who looked at her that way? A man who loved her so much he could live with her infertility?

For an instant Brady's face flitted across her mind. Kirsten shook the image away as she forced herself not to think about the man who was invading her thoughts more often than she would like.

She had seen Cora and Brady briefly while they were standing on the portico. He had commandeered one of the golf carts that security used in order to give Cora a ride.

Kirsten almost hadn't recognized him as he helped Cora with her walker. He'd shaved and gotten a haircut, and he couldn't have looked better even if he was wearing a custom-tailored suit rather than one he'd borrowed from her dad. They were sitting somewhere behind her now—out of sight, but not out of mind.

After the bride and groom said the last vow, they kissed. The folks in the pews responded with loud applause and cheers. Kirsten went through the reception line on the portico. Afterward she followed the crowd across the quad, where white lights illuminated the fountain and some kind of sparkly stuff circulated in the water that flowed down each tier. White balloons attached to the fountain swayed in the gentle breeze. The photographer took photos of the wedding party with that image as the backdrop while the guests made their way to the reception being held in the senior-center cafeteria.

Brady walked beside Cora, who was doing famously with her walker. Her lavender dress shimmered in the overhead lights. She was a princess, and Brady was her handsome prince. Kirsten tried not to let her gaze follow the duo across the room, but her attention was drawn to Brady against her will. She couldn't ignore the thoughtfulness he showed toward his grandmother as he helped her find a seat at one of the tables that sported white tablecloths, place settings for eight and centerpieces consisting of white baskets filled with a rainbow of flowers.

"Brady sure looks good in a suit," Jen whispered.

Kirsten frowned. "Let's not talk about Brady."

"Then you've got to quit looking in his direction." Jen raised her eyebrows. "I've also noticed the way you look at him when he drops in to see Cora."

Kirsten couldn't argue. She'd met Brady less than two weeks ago, but in that short time she'd come to anticipate his daily visits. He flirted with her. He'd given her flowers. He made her feel special, like she was the only woman in his world, even when she knew he'd be flirting with whatever woman crossed his path next. He gave his full attention to whomever he was talking to at the time. Just as he was doing with Cora right now.

Kirsten found her place card on a nearby table and motioned to Jen. "We're over here at the same table."

"Good." Jen pulled out her chair as a smattering of applause crescendoed into raucous cheering for the wedding party.

Kirsten turned toward the door and sighed as she watched the happy couple. "Annie's so beautiful."

"Brides are beautiful." Jen gently poked Kirsten in the ribs. "I think you should be the next one."

Kirsten swatted at Jen. "Don't say that too loudly. My dad might hear it. I managed to keep him from finding me a date."

Laughing, Jen winked. "What's he going to think when you catch the bouquet?"

"I'm not catching the bouquet. It's Melody's turn." Kirsten nodded toward Melody, who was the maid of honor.

"I might put in a word with the bride to aim in your direction." Jen grinned.

Kirsten ignored her comment as the wedding party took their places at the head table. Jordan Montgomery— Ian's father—offered a prayer of thanks for the meal. After Kirsten went through the line and returned to her seat, she tried not to let her gaze wander toward Brady and Cora. The laughter coming from Cora's friends told Kirsten that Brady was probably telling one of his jokes.

As the wedding party finished their meal, one of Ian's brothers, his dad and Melody gave toasts to the happy couple. By the time they were done, very few guests had dry eyes. Ian and Annie's story had touched a lot of people at The Village.

After the toasts, a DJ cued up a song and asked the

bride and groom to come out for the first dance. Boisterous applause accompanied their walk to the open space in the cafeteria that would serve as a dance floor. As the first notes of "God Gave Me You" filled the room, Ian took Annie in his arms, and they glided across the floor together. When they finished, there was more applause. They had several more specialty dances with their parents and Kara and Spencer. Then the DJ invited everyone to dance.

When Jen and Scott got up to dance, Kirsten looked across the room. Her heart melted at the sight of Brady dancing with Cora. Cora's broad smile could have illuminated the room. Kirsten didn't want to be reminded of how she'd badly misjudged Brady in regard to his grandmother. Had she misjudged him in other areas, as well?

The slow dance ended, and a fast-paced song followed right on its heels. The lively song sent many oldsters to their seats and brought a younger crowd to the dance floor. After several dances, the DJ announced that the bride and groom were ready to cut the cake. After several more songs, Ian got ready to throw the garter. Kirsten watched in amazement as her dad joined the crowd of single men.

When the garter sailed high over the heads of the men at the front and her dad snatched it, Kirsten stood there with her mouth open. Watching the guys teasing him, she shook her head in amazement. Her dad was full of surprises tonight. He'd even brought a date, Debra McCoy, one of the ladies from an area church who volunteered at The Village store each week.

As the men dispersed, Kirsten's dad stood there talking to Brady. What were they talking about? Weddings? Sports? Her? She shouldn't feel so full of herself that she would think they would discuss her. While she wondered about their conversation, they headed her way.

"Hey, Dad, I didn't know you were bringing a date." Kirsten smiled, trying to calm her racing heart as she looked at Brady.

"I thought I'd bring one since you didn't." Adam smiled as he raised his eyebrows.

"And you caught the garter." Kirsten couldn't keep the incredulity out of her voice.

"Yeah, I thought I'd show all those younger guys how it's done." Her dad's smile broadened into a grin as he clapped Brady on the back. "Brady and I have been talking about a job for him at the nursing home."

Kirsten tried not to let her mouth hang open. "At the nursing home?"

"Yeah, I was a medic in the army."

Kirsten didn't know what to make of this new information. Brady had said very little about his time in the army during any of their conversations. "What kind of a job?"

"An aide. It's only temporary until I can find something that pays better."

"Super." Kirsten glanced at Brady. "That'll make Cora happy."

Brady turned to look at Cora. "She's already so happy she can hardly stand it. Being here has been great therapy for her."

Before Kirsten could respond, Jen came over and dragged her out to the dance floor, where Annie was getting ready to throw her bouquet. "I've put in a good word for you," Jen said with a wink.

Kirsten frowned. "I'm not going to make an effort for this bouquet."

Jen ignored her and waved as she backed away. "Good luck."

Still frowning, Kirsten shook her head. She stood there as she watched the younger women jostle for position as Annie looked over the group. She was obviously looking for her intended target. Kirsten surmised it wasn't her when Annie focused her gaze on Melody, her enthusiasm for this exercise clearly matching Kirsten's.

Melody had lost her fiancé several years ago when he was killed while delivering aid to people in Afghanistan—a senseless tragedy. Since that time, she'd thrown herself into her work and had been much like Kirsten—dateless.

Finally, Annie turned her back to the group and let the bouquet fly. The bunch of flowers missed Kirsten and landed at Melody's feet. Several young ladies scrambled to snatch the bouquet right out from under Melody. When the cluster of women dispersed, Kayla, one of the young nurse's aides, emerged, all smiles, as she held the flowers high. Melody grinned and congratulated the younger woman.

Melody turned to Kirsten. "Someone's happy."

"I would say so." Kirsten chuckled. "I think Annie intended that for you."

Melody nodded. "Yeah, but I told her I wasn't making an effort to get it."

"That's what I told Jen. She was pushing for me to snag it."

"It's bad being single around this place. Everyone is out to fix us up with someone." Melody laughed.

While Kirsten and Melody chatted, the DJ started the music again. The notes of a slow song prompted several couples to head for the dance floor. Kirsten's stomach took a dive when she met Brady's gaze as he headed her way.

"You didn't try very hard for that bouquet. I could give you lessons on how to catch, so you'll be ready for the next wedding."

Shaking her head, Kirsten laughed halfheartedly. "Thanks, but no thanks."

"How about a dance instead?" The green flecks in his golden-brown eyes seemed to prance with mischief.

"I'd love to. Much more fun than learning how to catch." Despite all her reservations, this was what she'd been looking forward to all evening, and she wasn't sure why.

Before she had a chance to say anything else, Brady put an arm around her waist as he guided her to the music. "I was hoping sometime tonight we'd get a chance to do this."

Kirsten's heart fluttered. She tried to focus her attention on something besides herself. "How's Cora holding up? I hope she's not getting too tired."

Brady glanced at Cora. "She told me she'd tell me if she did, so I hope she's true to her promise. She's excited to be with her friends. Besides, I was told she had to be back in her room by nine o'clock at the latest. We'll see if she lasts that long."

Kirsten looked up at Brady. "I know she misses the weekly dominoes and bridge at the senior center. Some of her friends come over during the week and play cards with her, but it's not the same."

When the song ended and another slow number began, Brady didn't relinquish his hold on her. "One more dance?"

"Okay." Kirsten nodded. "So when do you start work?"

"Nothing's official." Brady shrugged. "But I asked to work the evening shift. That way I can look for something that pays better during the day. And there's a bonus. I get to work with you."

Kirsten gave him a wry smile. "Are you sure that's a bonus?"

"Sure. I'll teach all the late-shift folks how to have fun."

"You mean you don't think we have fun now?"

"No, I didn't mean that, just that it will be twice as much fun with me around."

Shaking her head, Kirsten chuckled. "I'll take your word for it. With your medic's background, aren't you qualified for something more than an aide?"

"You'd think so, but that's not the case."

"Why?"

"Even though medics know and perform a lot of medical procedures, we don't have the certification required for higher-paying civilian medical jobs like paramedics. Our training isn't licensed."

Kirsten didn't know what to think about the whole situation. "Is that why you worked on oil rigs and fishing boats?"

Brady nodded. "The pay was definitely better."

"Well, I hope things work out for you."

"Me, too." He stepped away as the song ended. "Thanks for the dance. I'd better check on Cora."

"I'd like to say hi to Cora, too."

Brady gestured toward the table where Cora sat with her friends. "Be my guest, but please don't tell her about our job-search conversation. I don't want to create any expectations. I'll tell her when I'm ready to start."

"Absolutely."

"Thanks."

When Cora saw Kirsten and Brady coming, she smiled broadly and waved. Kirsten reached the table first. Leaning over, she gave Cora a hug. "Are you enjoying the party?"

"It's been marvelous." Cora clapped her hands together. "The best time I've had in years."

Kirsten patted the older lady's shoulder. "I'm glad."

"I'm doing fabulously with my friends." Cora looked up at Brady. "You looked like you were having fun dancing. Why don't you run along with the younger people for a while?"

"Are you sure, Gram?" Brady flashed his signature grin. "You aren't going to talk about me while I'm gone, are you?"

Cora chuckled. "You ears might be burning. Go enjoy another dance with Kirsten. You two look good together."

A chorus of agreement rose from the table of seniors. Kirsten had no doubt they were trying their best to do some matchmaking. She looked over at Brady. His expression gave no clue as to his thoughts. She couldn't figure out if his previous teasing about dates was just flirting or whether he was seriously pursuing her. His intensions weren't clear. Her poor track record with men made her cautious, especially with guys like Brady, who liked to charm his way through life.

"Okay, Ms. Bailey, they want to see us dance. So let's give them a show." Brady took Kirsten's hand and led her to the dance floor.

"So, you like to dance?"

"Not necessarily, but it gives me an excuse to be with a pretty woman."

Kirsten refused to comment on his statement. More flirting. That's all it was to him. Why couldn't she get that through her brain? Did she want it to be more? No. When she was with him, he exasperated her, and she wished he'd go away. But when he wasn't with her, she exasperated herself, wishing he were. She would survive. Cora would be happy. And Brady would be…what? His sometimes-annoying, charming, handsome self. She'd better put a brick wall around her heart, or she was in big, big trouble.

Why was she even thinking about a relationship with anyone? Her first priority was going back to Brazil. But the difficulty in getting her visa left her wondering what God wanted for her, wondering whether her dad was right that she should stay here.

She had purposely avoided dating because of her intention to go back to her mission work. A serious relationship just wouldn't work unless that person was as committed as she was to going to the mission field. Brady hated big cities and closed-in spaces. São Paulo, where she worked in Brazil, was all of that. But wasn't she getting way ahead of herself? Even if those obstacles weren't in the way of a relationship with him, what would he think about her inability to have children?

As the last notes faded and the next song blared over the speakers, Ruby appeared near them and motioned to Brady. He hurried toward her as Kirsten followed close behind.

Ruby cupped her hands around her mouth. "Cora's getting tired. I think you should take her back to her room."

"Sure thing. I'll see about rounding up a golf cart." Brady hurried toward the exit.

Ruby let out a sigh. "Cora hated to disturb you and Brady, but I don't want her to exert herself too much."

Kirsten nodded. "You were right to tell him."

"You know she's hatching every plan in the book to get you and Brady together." Ruby gave Kirsten a knowing look.

"I kind of guessed that." Kirsten wanted to say Cora shouldn't get her hopes up, but she kept that to herself as she walked with Ruby over to see the woman in question.

When they reached the table where she sat, Ruby looked down at her friend. "Brady's getting the golf cart to take you back to your room."

Cora nodded. "I hate for the fun to end, but these old bones need some rest."

In minutes Brady reappeared. "Gram, the golf cart is waiting."

"I'm ready." With Brady's assistance, she pushed herself to her feet.

Kirsten watched as Brady helped Cora to the door. Kirsten didn't want to let him tie her in knots, but she didn't know how to act around him. She'd formed a negative opinion of him because he'd never answered his phone calls, and her initial meeting with him hadn't served to change her mind. But she'd been wrong about Brady. Everything about the past few days confirmed that she'd been mistaken. He might be rough around the edges, but he was a good guy who loved his grandmother.

How was she supposed to figure out the right path for her life? She wanted to go back to Brazil, but that was on hold. She was attracted to Brady, but she couldn't take him seriously. Her father was suddenly dating.

All of these changes and complications created a sense of unrest. They unsettled her and made her question everything she wanted from life. She'd spent years on the mission field relying on God's guidance. Unexpectedly her world was adrift with doubt. She wanted to see God's plan, but the path wasn't clear. Would she find the right way or continue to drift?

Dark clouds obscured the setting sun as Kirsten parked her car in her dad's driveway. Since she'd moved out on her own, whenever she had a weekend off, her dad was sure to invite her over for at least one meal. She always looked forward to chatting with him, but tonight would be different with Brady there. She sat in the car a moment and prepped herself to face the two men who had occupied a lot of her thoughts lately.

Her dad probably had no clue that Brady had indicated his interest in her. Was Brady's interest only a tease? He never seemed truly serious. He was always flirting and joking around. What could she take away from his behavior?

She wished she could figure it out, but what difference did it make when she wanted to return to Brazil? With the long wait on the visa, her doubts about getting to go back continued to grow. Missionary visas had become increasingly hard to get. She should quit worrying and live one day at a time and know God had a plan for her. He knew exactly what she needed and where she should be.

As she walked toward the house, thunder rumbled in the distance. Kirsten didn't bother to knock but went right into the house. "Dad, I'm here."

"We're in the kitchen." Her dad's voice sounded from the back of the house.

She traipsed through the living room, passing by the dining room, where the table was set with the good china. The delicious smell of garlic, tomato and spices wafting from the kitchen made her mouth water. What was going on? Was her dad actually cooking? Brady had said her dad had fixed him a couple of meals, but actually seeing him do it was something new.

When she reached the kitchen doorway, the sight before her stopped her in her tracks. Her dad stood in front of the stove as he stirred something in a pot. Debra McCoy was chopping romaine on a cutting board, and Brady was slicing a large loaf of Italian bread.

He looked up and grinned at her. "You're in for a treat tonight."

A sinking sensation hit her right in the midsection as she watched him. She took a moment to gather her thoughts. "Who's the head chef?"

"Brady." Her dad and Debra both spoke at once.

Kirsten frowned. "Debra is a guest. Why is she making the salad?"

Debra looked up. "I volunteered."

"Do you need me to do something?" Kirsten looked over at Brady as he popped the bread into the toaster oven.

"No, we're good. Everything will be ready in about ten minutes." Brady went over to the stove and took the lid off a pot of boiling water and put a package of spaghetti in it, then looked over at her. "Want something to drink?"

"No thanks. I'll have water when we eat."

Kirsten watched and marveled at Brady's command. She'd never imagined him as a chef, or even being halfway proficient in the kitchen. As the men finished with the final preparations, she helped herself to some water.

When she turned toward the dining room, Brady came up behind her. "I could've gotten that for you."

She looked at the bowl Brady carried. "Did you make the sauce, or is it out of a jar?"

He placed the bowl of sauce on the table, then feigned a hurt look. "You think I would serve you sauce out of a jar?"

Kirsten shrugged. "I use sauce out of a jar all the time."

He leaned closer and lowered his voice. "I do, too, but tonight I wanted to impress you with my culinary skills."

"You are impressing me." Kirsten pulled out a chair.

"Then my plan is working."

After everyone was seated, Adam said a prayer. As

they passed the food, Kirsten wasn't sure what the evening would hold. She took a bite of the spaghetti, then looked over at Brady. "This is really good."

"What did you expect?" He raised his eyebrows as he looked at her.

"You made this from scratch?" she asked, amazed at how good it was.

Brady looked over at her dad. "Tell her how I've been slaving in the kitchen all afternoon."

Adam nodded. "That's right. He chopped and stirred and tasted."

"I believe you. It just surprises me." Kirsten shook her head. "I don't know too many men who cook, other than on a grill."

"I can do that, too." Brady's signature grin appeared.

Kirsten didn't have a response as her stomach did that little flip-flop that so often happened when Brady grinned at her. As they ate, the group talked about getting ready for the fall festival. When the guys started talking about local sports, Kirsten and Debra discussed the volunteer work she did at The Village store.

"How are things working out now that you have a real storefront instead of a room on campus?" Kirsten asked.

"It makes for a little more work, but it's a valuable fund-raising tool as well as making people more aware of what y'all do at The Village."

"We're so thankful for volunteers like you." Kirsten took a sip of her water.

"I'm glad I can help." Debra smiled. "We could always use more helpers. We've had a lot of donations lately, and we're behind putting them out on the sales floor."

"Where's the store?" Brady asked.

"In a strip mall down the road from The Village."

Kirsten gave him a curious glance. "Do you plan to do some shopping?"

"No, I thought I'd volunteer to help until I start work." Brady looked over at Debra. "Who should I contact?"

"Fantastic. Melody Hammond usually coordinates the volunteers." Debra looked over at Kirsten. "Is that right?"

"Yes." Kirsten nodded her head as a loud clap of thunder sounded nearby, following a flash of lightning. "That was loud. Sounds like we're in for a storm."

"We can always use the rain, but I hate thunderstorms." Debra shook her head.

When the meal was over, Brady stood and picked up his plate. "Time to start the cleanup."

Kirsten grabbed her plate and her dad's. "Let me help."

"You sit and relax." Brady took the plates from her.

"But—"

"No buts."

Kirsten stared at him with her mouth agape.

Brady chuckled. "You can close your mouth now."

"I'm going to help whether you like it or not." She picked up some serving dishes and joined Brady in the kitchen.

Brady turned as she put the bowls on the counter next to the sink. "Can't stay away?"

Kirsten glanced toward the dining room, where her dad and Debra were talking. "If I help, that gives my dad and Debra some time alone."

Brady looked that way, too, then back at Kirsten. "Okay, for the sake of a budding relationship, I'll let you into my kitchen."

"Your kitchen?"

"Yes, I've taken over the cooking duties at least until I start work at the nursing home."

"And when will that be?"

"Not sure." Brady started loading the dishwasher. "They're still processing my paperwork. You know, background checks and the like."

"Yes, I had to go through that, too." Kirsten put the leftover food in containers and put them in the refrigerator.

Brady raised his eyebrows as he ran water in the sink. "Even you?"

"Everyone has to go through a background check. The Village takes security and safety very seriously."

Brady nodded as he washed and rinsed a pan, then put it in the drying rack. "That's for sure, and I'm glad they do."

"What about you? Do you ever take anything seriously?" Eyeing Brady, Kirsten dried the pan and wondered what his response to her question would be.

"Yeah, three things. My faith, Cora and getting a date with you."

Before Kirsten could say anything, thunder boomed and a streak of lightning illuminated the night sky. "Wow! That was really close."

"Yeah, it's pouring out there now." Brady looked out the window as Adam's phone started playing "When the Saints Go Marching In."

Adam rushed into the kitchen and answered his phone. No one said a thing. The color drained from his face while he listened to the caller.

When he ended the call, Kirsten asked, "Dad, what's wrong?"

Adam let out a harsh breath. "One of the children's homes was struck by lightning. The strike started a fire on the roof. They called the fire department, but before they got there, one end of the house collapsed."

"Was anyone hurt?" Fearing gripping her, Kirsten pressed her lips together.

Adam shook his head. "Everyone got out safely. We can be thankful for that, but I need to get to the campus so I can help figure out what to do with the displaced house parents and kids."

Kirsten picked up her purse and jacket. "Dad, let me give you a ride since my car's the last one in the drive. That way we don't have to jockey the vehicles."

"Good idea." Adam turned to Debra. "I'm sorry to have to run."

"That's no problem. I want to help, too," Debra said.

"Me, too." Brady grabbed his jacket out of the coat closet.

Adam surveyed the group. "Thanks for your help. I appreciate anything you can do."

A somber mood stifled conversation as Kirsten drove toward The Village. Adam and Debra sat in the back while Brady joined Kirsten in the front seat. Although the rain had subsided, the headlights reflected on the wet roads. An occasional sprinkle splatted on the windshield, and sporadic rumbles of thunder filled the quiet.

While Kirsten drove, she thanked God that everyone was safe. She prayed the damage from the fire would be minimal. Her problems and concerns about Brady and even her unease about what the future held seemed trivial compared to what the residents of the burned house faced. She had to focus on others' needs and not on herself. God had a plan, and she wanted to fit into it no matter where it led her.

Chapter Six

Flashing red-and-white lights atop a fire engine illuminated the night sky as Brady strode across the campus, dodging puddles as he went. Kirsten and Debra walked nearby while Adam talked on his phone. The acrid smell of smoke filled the air. In front of a barricade, a group of people huddled in the street.

When Adam finished talking on the phone, Melody stepped out of the group and came toward them. "Thanks for coming so soon."

"Tell me what happened." Concern painted Adam's face.

"The Dunns said their family was watching a video when a loud clap of thunder sounded. They saw a blinding flash of lightning. The lights went out, and the next thing they knew they realized the house was on fire." Melody pointed upward. "You can see where the roof burned and collapsed on that end of the house."

"Is the fire under control?" Adam asked.

"Yes, but we'll have to wait until morning to see how much damage there is." Melody grimaced.

Melody and Adam continued to talk as Brady stood off to one side, waiting to see how he could help. He glanced over at the Dunns, who had their charges huddled around them as they tried to comfort the children. A couple of the younger ones were crying. Adam and Melody conferred with the Dunns.

Brady bowed his head and prayed for peace in his life and peace in the lives of those who'd lost their home. He knew what it was like to be homeless. At least this family wouldn't have to live on the streets. When he raised his head, Adam and Melody were coming his way.

Adam motioned to Brady and Kirsten. "Kirsten, I want Brady and you to take Zach and Tyler back to my house. They can stay in the spare room on the lower level." Adam looked directly at Brady. "The boys said they knew you, so I figured that would be helpful in their transition."

Brady nodded. "Are they okay?"

"A little shaken and fearful they've lost some prized possessions, but we can't go into the house until we get the okay from the fire department." Adam's mouth formed a grim line. "Kirsten can help you get things settled."

"Dad, do they have any of their possessions?" Kirsten asked.

Adam shook his head. "You'll need to stop at a store on your way home and pick up some pajamas, a change of clothes and toiletries for them."

"I think we're going to have a long night." Melody sighed. "Your dad and Debra are going to stay and help me decide where to house everyone else. I'll give your dad and Debra a ride home. Thanks for taking Zach and Tyler."

"Glad to do it." Kirsten gave Melody a hug, then hugged her dad. "I'll call for an update after we get the boys settled. See you later."

"Okay." Adam waved.

Kirsten joined Brady, and they walked over to Zach and Tyler. "How do you know those little boys?"

"One day when I was going to see Cora, I saw them kicking around a soccer ball on the quad. I stopped to talk and did a few passes with them."

Kirsten smiled at him. "You're just like Cora. You've never met a stranger."

"I hope that's good."

"It is."

With Kirsten's praise following him, Brady hunkered down next to the boys. "Hey, guys. Guess you're going home with me tonight. You cool with that?"

The boys nodded, their little faces solemn in the dim light.

Brady put a hand on the boys' shoulders as he stood between them. "Let me introduce you to Ms. Kirsten."

Kirsten stepped forward and looked at the boys. "I hear you like to play soccer."

"How'd you know?" Tyler wrinkled his freckled nose.

"I told her." Brady ruffled Tyler's reddish brown hair. "This is Tyler, and this guy over here is Zach. Ms. Kirsten is a nurse over at the nursing home, and she helps take care of my grandmother."

Zach and Tyler said nothing else, only nodded, as they followed Brady and Kirsten toward her car. Flickers of lightning still flashed in the distance. The stench of the fire lingered in the air. When they reached the vehicle, Brady opened the door to let the boys into the backseat and they hopped inside.

No one said much of anything as they left campus. Brady wondered about the boys' silence as they rode to the nearby big-box store. Were they worried about a strange new living situation? Brady didn't know their circumstances, but this was another upheaval in the lives of two little boys who had obviously already suffered family turmoil of some kind. He hoped he could soothe their fears and help them adjust to unfamiliar circumstances.

The boys still didn't say much as they picked out what they needed for the night. Heading toward the checkout, they went by a display that featured soccer balls. Brady grabbed one.

Kirsten looked at him as he put the ball on the conveyor belt at the checkout. "For the boys or you?"

"Both." Brady chuckled as he glanced down at Zach and Tyler. "Would you guys like to play soccer after school while you're staying with Mr. Adam and me?"

Smiles covered both little faces as the boys nodded, but they still remained unusually quiet on the ride to Adam's house. When they arrived, the group trooped inside with their packages. Still not talking, Zach and Tyler followed Kirsten as she led them down the stairs in the split-level house. She opened a door on the left-hand side of the room that Brady had always assumed was storage.

"Here's where you're going to stay. You can decide which bed you want."

Zach raced into the room and dumped his bag on the twin bed farthest from the door. "I get this one."

Tyler eyed his brother as he stood there holding the plastic shopping bag to his chest. "Why do you get to choose first?"

"'Cause I'm oldest."

"So? That doesn't mean you can choose first."

"Does so." Zach sat on the bed and crossed his arms.

The atmosphere had gone from quiet to argumentative. Surprised by the change in the boys, Brady wasn't sure what to do as he stood in the doorway. He'd been an only child and had had very little interaction with kids throughout his life. Since Kirsten had worked with kids in Brazil, did she know how to handle the situation?

Just then she looked over at him, her eyebrows raised in a question. Could he help her? Brady stepped into the room and took a position between the beds covered in navy-and-white plaid quilts. He looked at Zach. "Is there a special reason why you want this bed rather than the other one?"

Zach pressed his lips together as a defiant look radiated from his eyes. Refusing to answer, he looked from Brady to Kirsten. Brady wondered who was going to win the showdown. Had the displacement because of the fire caused the boys to act out?

Brady tried to think back to his own behavior when his mom had died. He'd been angry and sullen. He wasn't sure how these boys had come to live at The Village. They probably had a different experience, but could they be having some of the same feelings he'd experienced?

Kirsten looked over at Tyler. "Is there any reason why you want the bed your brother has chosen?"

Tyler's lower lip began to quiver as he looked at Kirsten. Shaking his head, he lowered his gaze. Brady's heart went out to the younger boy as he slunk down on the bed nearest him, still holding the bag to his chest. His shoulders began to shake, but he made no sound.

Brady eyed Zach, who appeared unrepentant. Brady wanted to reprimand the kid and ask him if he was happy that he'd made his little brother cry. But that definitely wasn't the best strategy, especially seeing the fear in the boy's eyes.

Kirsten quickly joined Tyler on the bed and slipped an arm around his shoulders, then hugged him. She didn't say anything, just held him close and patted his back. When his shoulders quit shaking, he looked up at

Kirsten, a gulp bobbing his Adam's apple. "How long do we have to stay here?"

Kirsten shrugged. "That all depends on how much damage your house has."

Tyler sniffled. "But I miss the Dunns."

"I know you do, Tyler, but I think you'll like it here with Mr. Adam and Mr. Brady." Kirsten looked over at Brady.

Brady's heart thumped against his rib cage as he sat next to Tyler. "I know you're going to miss your family at The Village, but Mr. Adam and I will try our best to make things good for you here until you can go back. I'm looking forward to playing soccer with you guys."

Tyler's face brightened. "Me, too."

Zach hopped off the other bed. "Me, too."

Kirsten glanced over at the older boy. "Zach, do you think the Dunns would be happy with the way you've acted here this evening?"

"No." Zach hung his head.

"Do you have something you'd like to say to your brother?" Brady asked.

Zach shuffled closer to where Tyler sat. "Sorry."

Tyler didn't say anything as he stared wide-eyed at his brother.

Brady held his breath as Kirsten gave Tyler a little nudge and raised her eyebrows as she looked at him, her eyes full of apprehension.

"Okay. You're forgiven." His mouth twisted, making a half pout and half smile.

Kirsten hopped up from the bed. "Now that we have that settled, let me show you where everything is."

Brady watched while Kirsten traipsed around the room, pointing out the dresser and chest and showing them the connected full bath. She knew where everything was located. He liked how they had worked as a team to deal with the kids. Had she also noticed how well they got on together?

She stood to the side of the doorway and motioned for the boys to go into the bathroom. "You can put your toothbrushes in the holder and the toothpaste in the medicine cabinet. Your other toiletries can go in there or in the drawer next to the sink."

After they put their things in the bathroom, they returned to the bedroom and retrieved their shopping bags. Without a hint of an argument, the boys picked out a drawer to put their new belongings in. Brady smiled as he leaned against the door frame.

After they'd put everything away, Kirsten looked over at Brady. "Since it's a weekend and the boys don't have school tomorrow, can you find something they might like to watch in my dad's DVD collection?"

Brady nodded. "Sure."

"While you do that, I'll give my dad a call and see what's going on." Kirsten extracted her phone from her purse.

"Good idea." Brady went into the adjoining room.

A flat-screen TV sat on a stand on the far wall. A sectional covered in some kind of brownish-tan fabric hugged the opposite wall and curved into the room, creating a divider between the main part of the room and an area that contained a desk and computer. He searched through the DVDs during Kirsten's call. She said very little as she listened to Adam's report.

She looked his way as she ended the call. "Good news— they've got a place for everyone to stay. Bad news—they can't get in to the house, and the firefighters told them that even the things that weren't burned will have smoke and water damage. So we don't know what, if anything, will be salvageable."

"Can they put out a call for donations for the family?" Brady asked.

Kirsten nodded. "Dad said such an announcement would go out first thing in the morning. Churches will rally. He's going to be helping get everyone settled and said he won't be home for a while."

"That means we have time to watch one of these movies." Brady held up three as he looked at the boys. "I've got *The Incredibles*, *The Karate Kid* or *Chariots of Fire*. Which one do we watch?"

"What are they about?" Zach asked.

"I'll give you a summary of each movie. Then you can decide." Brady proceeded to read the information on the DVD cases. When he finished, he looked at the boys and hoped they wouldn't argue about this. If he gave them a suggestion, maybe they'd take it. "If I got to choose, I'd probably pick *The Karate Kid*."

Zach and Tyler looked at each other and nodded, then scrambled to find a seat on the sectional.

Brady turned to Kirsten. "Are you going to join us?"

"I'll make some popcorn while you get everything ready. Okay?"

"Works for me." Brady placed the DVD in the player and turned on the TV.

By the time the beginning credits were rolling across the screen, Kirsten returned, the smell of buttered popcorn accompanying her as she set a large bowl on the coffee table. She set a stack of smaller bowls next to the big one. "Help yourselves."

The boys dug in immediately, then settled back to enjoy the movie. The only light in the darkened room came from the TV. Brady looked up at Kirsten as she stood at the end of the sectional. He felt like a high school kid again, wishing the cute girl in his math class would sit by him at lunch. He patted the space next to him. "This spot is reserved just for you."

She didn't acknowledge his statement but filled a bowl with popcorn and handed it to him. He silently mouthed his thanks. Then she scooped up a bowlful for herself and settled beside him. Did he dare put an arm around her shoulders? No. He didn't want to make one move too many. For the next two hours, he sat next to the woman who was capturing his heart bit by bit. He was afraid he couldn't bring himself to let her go, especially to a far-away place like Brazil. How could he change her mind about going back?

Was he going to let her walk away? He used to fight for what he wanted, but then he'd never been fighting for the attention of a woman. Maybe he'd been a coward when it came to women, but he wasn't a quitter. Today was teaching him that he really did care about her and wanted her to care about him.

After the movie ended, Brady instructed the boys to get ready for bed while Kirsten put away the DVD. After Zach and Tyler had put on their pajamas and brushed their teeth, she stood next to Brady while the boys said their prayers. Then they hopped into bed, and Kirsten tucked them in.

Brady couldn't help thinking about the domestic scene they painted. What would it be like to have a family with Kirsten? He shook the question away. He couldn't go there. He tried to keep his thoughts in check as he said good-night to Zach and Tyler. Despite all his wishes, he didn't see much hope for changing their very different plans for the future. But the future didn't lie in his hands—it was in God's hands—and Brady was slowly learning that God's plan was always better.

"Mr. Brady, could you leave the door open?" Zach called out as Brady put his hand on the doorknob.

"Sure." Brady followed Kirsten up the stairs. "I can tell you've worked with kids. You were marvelous tonight."

Turning, she gave him an impish smile. "Aren't I always?"

"Yeah. Guess you are." He let a grin slide into place.

"Actually, we made a pretty good team."

"I was thinking the same thing. That must mean you're ready to agree to go out with me."

Her eyes twinkled as she looked at him "You aren't going to take no for an answer, are you?"

"No." Was she flirting with him? With every nerve standing at attention, he swallowed hard. He wanted to kiss her more than anything, but she probably wouldn't take kindly to that move, especially with the boys not far away. He didn't want to jeopardize his chances for getting that date. He mustered all his resolve and walked to the other side of the living room couch. Distance provided safety.

Kirsten looked at him as if she knew why he'd walked away. Or was it his imagination? Paranoia was not his friend. Brady glanced toward the stairway. "Do you think the boys will have any trouble sleeping?"

"I hope not, but Dad's good with that kind of stuff if you're concerned about it."

Brady gave her a half smile, apprehension over dealing with two little boys roiling his gut. "I don't have much experience with kids, but I've always thought I'd like to have kids someday. So this will be a good experience."

"It will. They seemed pretty excited about getting to play soccer with you."

"True." Brady wondered about the sadness that crept across Kirsten's features. Was she worried about how everyone would handle the upheaval?

"I'm sure you and Dad will be able to manage whatever comes up." Kirsten grabbed the popcorn bowls, then turned toward the kitchen. "I'm going to clean these."

Brady followed Kirsten into the kitchen. Her confidence in him bolstered his ego. When she started to wash the big popcorn bowl, he grabbed a dish towel. Sharing dish duties with her put those domestic thoughts back into his mind. He tried to dismiss them again, but he wasn't sure he wanted them to go away. He liked the idea of being there for her no matter what the task.

Brady finished drying the bowl and put it in the cupboard. He turned, ready to bring up the date again. Before he could open his mouth, Adam walked into the kitchen.

"Dad, you're home. Did you get everything settled?"

Adam nodded. "We did as much as we could tonight."

"I'm sorry your evening with Debra was ruined."

"That is the least of my worries. Debra was a big help tonight. She's a good organizer." Adam glanced Brady's way. "So I hear you had to deal with a couple of unhappy boys."

"Yes, sir, but your daughter smoothed everything over. The boys are in bed."

"She's definitely good with kids." Adam patted Kirsten's shoulder, then gave her a kiss on the cheek.

"Thanks, Dad."

Adam nodded. "I'm worn out, so this old man is headed to bed. Good night."

"Good night." Kirsten gave her dad a hug.

"Good night, sir." Brady liked the way Kirsten related

to her dad. That, and the way she had handled the situation with the boys, reminded him of all the reasons he cared about the sometimes-prickly nurse with the soft heart. She was tough and tender all at the same time. How could he keep his own heart from wishing she didn't want to return to the mission field? Would a date make a difference, or was he fighting the inevitable? Whatever. He wasn't going to give up the fight.

"Thanks for your help tonight." Kirsten sighed. "I'd better head for home."

"Happy to, but before you go." Brady touched her arm. "I want to finish our earlier conversation."

Kirsten's brow knit in a little frown. "What conversation?"

"The one we were having when your dad got that phone call."

"You have to refresh my memory."

Brady gazed at Kirsten. Not good that she didn't remember. "You asked me about—"

"I remember." A smile curved her lips. "About being serious."

"Yes, I want to take you out." His heart hammered as he waited for her reply.

"And when would this date be?"

"Whenever you have a day off."

"And what if that doesn't correspond with your day off?"

"I don't have an official start date. And I have a feeling you might have some influence over the person in charge of the schedule."

Kirsten gave him a lopsided smile. "I just might. How about discussing it after you actually start work? Then we can look at a schedule."

"Okay. I'm going to hold you to that."

She held up one hand. "I'm not trying to change the conversation, but have you ever considered going back to school and getting a degree in nursing or becoming a physician's assistant?"

"Not really, especially not after I found out I could make big money working in the oil fields." Besides, after his experience on the battlefield, Brady wasn't sure he wanted to pursue medicine as a career. But he didn't want to admit that to Kirsten. As a medic, he'd seen a lot of horrific things—things he didn't want to think about.

He'd taken the work at the nursing home as a temporary stopgap on his way to something better, and it gave him a chance to work with Kirsten. His main focus now was Cora and her health. He wanted to be the grandson she deserved. Everything else came second.

"I think you should consider it. I've seen the way you interact with the residents even though you aren't even working there yet. You have a real knack with them."

Brady drank in Kirsten's praise. Should he consider it? "I'll think about it after I actually start work."

"Good." Kirsten slipped into her jacket and picked up her purse. "Are you coming to church with Dad in the morning?"

"I am. Let me walk you to your car." Brady wanted to spend every second with her that he could.

Kirsten shrugged. "Okay, but it's not necessary."

"But you never know if there might be puddles that I could keep you from stepping in by laying my jacket over them. I wouldn't want you to get your feet wet."

Kirsten laughed. "You know that's only a legend, don't you? Or should I call you Sir Brady Hewitt."

Brady joined in her laughter as he opened the door. "That sounds good. I'm your knight in shining armor.

And legend or no legend, I wouldn't want you to step in any puddles."

Kirsten laughed again as she stepped off the front porch. "Thanks for your concern."

Brady walked beside her, happy that she had tentatively agreed to go out with him. When she stopped beside her car, the streetlight illuminated her pretty features. He pushed his hands into the pockets of his jacket to keep from reaching out and pulling her to him for a kiss.

Kirsten unlocked her car. "I'll see you in the morning. Good night."

"Good night." He waved as she backed out of the driveway.

His breath created a cloud in the cool, dank air as Brady watched until her car disappeared from view. He turned and jogged to the house. Tonight his dreams were going to be filled with the images of a pretty nurse. But he had to temper his dreams with some common sense. He had to remember that Kirsten's dream was to return to Brazil. In the meantime he intended to make the best of it.

Monday afternoon, Brady sauntered down the nursing-home hallway carrying a large box in his arms. When he reached the nurses' station, he set the box on the counter and looked around for Kirsten. He'd seen her yesterday morning at church, but they hadn't had much chance to talk because she had been singing with the praise band and afterward had had a meeting with Melody.

Suddenly, Jen appeared from a storage room. "Hey, Brady. I hear you'll soon be roaming the halls here making all the little old ladies swoon with delight."

Brady let out a halfhearted chuckle. "Is that what I'm going to do?"

"You will brighten everyone's day."

"Well, right now I'm looking to brighten Kirsten Bailey's day. Know where I could find her?"

"With that box?" Jen asked.

"Hopefully with what's in the box." Brady tapped the side.

"Kirsten's making her rounds with the med cart. She should be back any minute."

True to Jen's word, a moment later, Kirsten rounded the corner as she pushed the cart ahead of her. When she saw him, she smiled, and Brady's heart did a little tap dance. He could hardly wait to show her what he'd brought her.

"Hey, Sir Hewitt, what you got there?"

"Something for you."

"For me?" She placed one hand over her heart as she came to a stop beside him. "What is it?"

"Something I picked up this morning at The Village store when I was helping Debra put things on the sales floor." Brady pushed the box down the counter toward Kirsten.

"What is it?" The wonder on Kirsten's face made Brady's day.

"Look inside and find out."

In her excitement, she fumbled to get the box open as she pulled off the tape holding it shut. An expression of awe spread across her face as she lifted the large clay pot out of the box. She looked at him as if he'd given her the world. "It's wonderful. How did you know I would like this?"

Brady shook his head. "I won't pretend I knew what this was, but Debra did. When I unpacked it, she told me that it was a *moqueca* pot used for making fish stew in Brazil. I immediately thought of you."

Kirsten ran a loving hand over the dark brown pot. "I had one of these when I was in Brazil, but I had to leave it behind when I came home."

"Then I'm glad I could replace it for you." Brady grinned. "I hope you're going to invite me over when you make *moqueca*."

"That's the least I can do to thank you for the gift. Next time I eat over at Dad's place, I'll make it for all of us." Kirsten gave him a hug. "Thanks so much."

Brady forced himself not to give any significance to the quick brotherly hug. "You're welcome."

Kirsten put the pot back in the box. "I can't believe there was one of these in The Village store."

Brady shrugged. "It was one of the donated items. Debra said that most likely someone who'd been to Brazil brought it home as a souvenir but never used it."

"She's probably right."

Brady tapped the top of the box. "Would you like me to take this to your car?"

"Ah, why don't you just take it with you when you go home? That way it'll be there when I come over to cook."

"That works for me. I'll take it to my pickup. Be back in a couple minutes." Brady trotted off with the image of Kirsten's joyous expression rolling through his mind.

When Brady returned, Kirsten was busy typing on her computer keyboard. He leaned on the counter and watched her. "I'll be starting work on Wednesday."

Kirsten looked up. "Yes. I see that you've been plugged in to take over for an aide who's on maternity leave."

"That's what I've been told." Brady continued to lean on the counter. "So do any of our days off coincide so I can take you on that date?"

Kirsten nodded. "I spoke without thinking the other

night. I'll be spending my days off preparing for the fall festival. But—"

"So we *do* have the same days off?" Brady grinned.

"Yes, seems that way."

"Looks like I'll be helping you prepare for the festival on those days, but afterwards we'll have our date."

"Let's just say we'll talk about it when it's over."

"Sure." Brady wasn't going to give her any hint that he was bothered by her apparent reluctance to go out with him. "That'll give me more time to plan something. You need to have a little more fun in your life."

"Speaking of fun. Are you and Dad enjoying your time with Tyler and Zach?"

"Those boys are keeping us both on our toes. Homework, playtime, baths and bedtime. But I'm lovin' it." Brady chuckled. "I'm getting a little taste of what Cora had to deal with when I was a kid. It makes me appreciate her even more."

"And you should."

"And on that note, I'm off to see that precious grandmother of mine." Brady saluted. "And don't forget we have a date in our future."

Brady sauntered down the hall toward Cora's room, forcing himself not to look back. Little by little he was finding a way into Kirsten's life. He hoped his initial attraction to the pretty nurse was only the beginning of something more. If he wanted to convince her that a relationship with him was a good thing, he was going to have to get to know her better. He had to find out why she was so determined to go back to Brazil when she had so many good things right here.

Chapter Seven

The following Saturday morning with the scent of freshly mowed grass filling the air, Kirsten walked toward the fountain, where she was supposed to meet Melody before going to the festival site to work. At the far end of the grassy expanse a group of youngsters chased a soccer ball. Her heart did a little jig when she noticed Brady yelling out encouraging instructions as he trotted down the field. As the group drew closer, Kirsten waved.

"Looks like you're all having fun," she called to him when he looked in her direction. She gave him a thumbs-up sign.

Brady nodded while he demonstrated a move to one of the girls, then loped over to Kirsten as the kids continued to play. "You're here early."

"So are you." Kirsten motioned to the group of kids. "Are you still planning to work on the festival today?"

Brady grinned. "I wouldn't miss a chance to work with you, but I brought Tyler and Zach over because the Dunns came to work on the house and brought the other kids. I thought the boys would enjoy seeing them. Then we started an impromptu game."

"The house parents will thank you for wearing them

out." Kirsten retrieved the ball that had careened out of bounds and handed it to Brady.

Brady gave the ball to a little girl, who passed it to a teammate. "Thanks."

"Nice that you have a connection with the kids." Kirsten could see how Brady related to the youngsters. Her dad had told her Zach and Tyler had taken to Brady and followed him around like lost puppies.

While the kids chased the ball down the field, Brady raced down the sidelines, still giving encouragement. Kirsten sighed as she continued to watch. Since the boys had moved in with her dad, Brady had shown her that he adored kids and kids adored him. She was growing to admire him greatly, too. What was she going to do when he brought up the date again? Would going out with him just be for fun, or would a date set up expectations? Maybe he had none. After all, he knew she wanted to go back to Brazil.

Sometimes, she just wanted to tell Brady to go away and leave her alone. She didn't want or have time for romance. But whenever he stood close, her heart told her something else. She had to admit that, from the beginning, he had garnered her awareness.

"Hey, Kirsten, are you ready to start the festival preparation?" Melody's question interrupted Kirsten's troubled thoughts.

"Yeah, whenever you are."

"Great." Melody turned as Brady joined them. "Hey, Brady.

Melody pointed toward the parking lot. "We're taking the van over to the festival site because I'm hauling some stuff. You and Brady are welcome to ride with me."

Kirsten took in Tyler's smudged face with his toothless smile as he raced up to Brady and tapped him on the arm.

"Mr. Brady, Zach scored a goal."

"Thanks for letting me know Tyler."

"You missed it." Tyler's words dripped with accusation.

"Yeah, I'm sorry, but I was talking to Ms. Kirsten." Brady blew his whistle and motioned for the kids to join him. As the group of eight gathered around Brady, eager faces gazed up at him. "Good job scoring the goal, Zach."

"Thanks." The boy's grin was as wide as his face.

"Y'all did terrific today." Brady surveyed the group. "Next week we'll work on passing, and then play a little like we did this morning."

"Aw, do we have to stop?" Zach stuck out his lower lip.

"Yep. Sorry, kids. I have to help with the festival booth."

"Can we help?" one of the little girls asked.

Brady looked over at Kirsten and Melody. "What do you think?"

"We can use all the help we can get, but we should check with their house parents." Melody whipped out her cell phone and made a few calls. When she finished, she nodded. "We're all set. They can join us."

As Brady led the gaggle of kids toward the van, Kirsten walked beside him. He had a way with them. They chattered and laughed as they hovered around him like flies at a picnic. He was obviously enjoying their liveliness. She liked that about him, but in the long run, it presented a problem for any future relationship with him. If they got closer, she'd have to eventually tell him the truth, that she couldn't have children. Her thinking was too far ahead of reality, and she tried to push the thought away. But Brady's constant reminder of their date kept thoughts of a relationship at the front of her mind.

When they arrived at the van, Brady opened the door

to the back, and the kids scrambled inside. Just as Kirsten started to get in, Melody came alongside. "I just had a phone call about a new arrival at the woman's shelter. I have to go over there before I go to the festival site. Will you drive the van? I'll come later."

"Sure." Kirsten nodded. "I think Brady and I can handle this group."

"Great." Melody hugged Kirsten and handed over the keys to the van. "Hopefully, I won't be too long."

Kirsten quickly explained the situation to Brady as she got behind the wheel.

Brady hopped into the front passenger seat and turned to look at the kids. "Everyone buckle your seat belts."

A chorus of "yes, sirs" rose from the backseats. As Kirsten maneuvered the van toward the entrance to The Village, a cacophony of laughter and questions filled the ten-minute trip to the church, where the festival was being held. Kirsten gave no-nonsense answers to the rapid-fire questions coming from the kids. By the time she parked the van, the kids and Brady knew exactly what to do.

The group scampered off the van and like good little soldiers paraded off with Brady toward a jumble of poles and canopies. He surveyed the mess, then glanced at Kirsten. "And where do you expect me to use a hammer?"

She tried for an annoyed look but failed as a smile threatened at the corners of her mouth. "The hammer comes later when we nail up the signs. These are supposed to fit together to form a booth. There are about a dozen more of these that have to be put together."

Brady picked up one of the poles. "Looks like we have a lot of work ahead of us."

Kirsten smiled halfheartedly as she motioned toward

the chaos. "I didn't realize these things had gotten so jumbled while they were in storage."

Brady nodded. "You do have a mess here. We need to have a plan in order to sort through this."

Kirsten eyed him. "Okay, I'm putting you in charge. Maybe the kids can help."

With a heavy sigh, Brady picked his way through the pieces, then turned to her. "When we take these down after the festival, we're going to label the parts. Then we won't have to go through this next year."

Kirsten nodded, unable to speak over the lump in her throat. Next year. Would she be here? If she had her visa, would she already be gone, like she'd planned? Why did the thought of not being here make her sad when her biggest dream for months had been to go back to Brazil?

Brady looked over the group of eager children. "Ms. Kirsten has told me to make a plan, so listen up, gang. Zach and Tyler, you're going to spread out the canopies."

The boys nodded and rushed over to the spot, their little chests puffed out with pride for the responsibility Brady had bestowed upon them. After getting the two boys set up with their job, Brady ushered the three girls with ponytails and high-pitched voices over to a spot where they could sort the various poles by size. He had the remaining boys sort the heavy-duty plastic pieces that connected the poles.

After Brady handed out all the assignments, he loped over to where Kirsten had just finished talking with a group of ladies who were hauling supplies into the all-purpose room of the church. "Anything I missed?"

"No. Looks like you've got all the kids busy with something. I knew you'd be a good organizer. I've seen that in your work at the nursing home."

"Praise from the not-so-prickly nurse." Brady grinned. "Does that mean you're going to go out with me?"

"Does that mean you've found my heart of gold?"

Brady let out a guffaw. "Must be since you're going out with me."

"I told you I can't commit to anything until after the festival. Why do you keep asking?"

"Just say yes, and I won't have to ask again."

Kirsten let out a heavy sigh as she rolled her eyes. Should she say yes and be done with it? He wasn't going to stop until she did. "Okay. Yes, I'll go out with you."

"Super!" Brady flashed his signature grin. "Now wasn't that easy?"

Kirsten chuckled. "Yes, but you have to promise me you won't mention it again until after the festival and after we see the next schedule."

"Yes, ma'am." Brady saluted. "I won't mention it again until the appointed time."

"Now we'd better check on the progress the kids have made." As Kirsten hurried toward the area where Zach and Tyler worked, she searched for some equilibrium as a hollow sensation zoned in on her stomach. Her nerves zinged. Had she just told Brady that she would go on a date with him? Right or wrong, she had finally made the decision. She hoped she wouldn't regret it.

Brady lengthened his strides to catch up to Kirsten. Was she already sorry she'd decided to go out with him? Had he badgered her until she had finally figured he'd leave her alone if she said yes? He shouldn't have doubts. He'd gotten what he wanted. Right now he had to help her with these booths, not think about what the future held.

Brady focused his attention on Zach and Tyler. "How's it going, guys?"

"There's still a big mess." Zach scrunched up his face as he held out his hands toward the canopies. "These things are too big, and we can't get them straight."

"We'll help you finish." Brady looked at Zach, then back at Kirsten.

Kirsten surveyed the work each group of children had done. "It's not as much of a mess as you think. All the other parts are ready, so we can start an assembly line to put this together."

The much-needed praise put smiles on the kids' faces. She not only had a tender heart for her patients at the nursing home, but she also had a tender heart for kids. Another thing to like about her.

Tyler picked up a pole. "Where does this go?"

"Right here." Brady pointed to a pocket in the canopy. "We put the right size pole here and then connect them."

A few moments after the group started their assembly line, Adam walked over. "How's everything going here?"

"Hey, Dad." Kirsten stopped working and looked at her father. "We're just starting to assemble the booths."

Adam grimaced. "We might need to put that on hold."

"Why?" A little pucker formed between Kirsten's eyebrows.

"I've just heard the weather forecast, and it's supposed to be blustery with a good chance of rain for the middle of the week." Adam rubbed the back of his neck as he gazed at Kirsten.

"Is the weather supposed to be bad on the day of the festival?" Kirsten asked.

Adam shook his head. "We have a good forecast for that day, but if we put these up now, I'm afraid the wind and rain could make a mess of the booths."

"Then what do we do with this stuff?" Kirsten gestured around the parking lot.

"We'll have to store it until Friday." Adam nodded toward the church building. "I'm going to check with the church staff and see what they suggest we do."

"Whatever you think is best." Kirsten looked over at the church building, a thread of worry once again wrinkling her brow. "We'll put everything on hold until you find out."

Brady wanted to reach out and smooth away her anxiety. He wanted to make everything right for her. But did that also include her getting that missionary visa? He didn't know how to answer that question. Part of him feared getting entangled in her life, only to have her leave. But that's exactly what he'd done by pushing for that date.

His heart hammered, and his stomach did cartwheels against his will. There was no denying his attraction to her. He liked the way she cared for her patients and the way she tried not to smile when he told one of his silly jokes. He even liked the way she frowned when she was irritated by something he said or did. It felt like falling in love.

What did he know about romantic love? He'd had no example from his parents. When his mother had been alive, she'd always seemed sad. His dad had been distant, and Brady feared that someday he might be like him. They'd hardly related as a couple. So he'd never seen it firsthand, but Chaplain Howard had taught him that love accepts the good and the bad.

That's how Jesus loves us, and that's how Christians are supposed to care for one another. Brady figured it was the same between a man and a woman. Could Kirsten learn to love the not-so-good stuff about him?

He shook the question away. Festival tents should occupy his mind. Even if he did finally have a date with

Kirsten, he wasn't ready to sort through his jumbled emotions.

Kirsten looked back toward the building, then turned to Brady. "Maybe we should put all the poles in the slots then roll up the canopies for storage."

Brady nodded. "Sounds like a good plan to me."

While they were rolling the canopies around the poles, Adam returned.

"So what did you find out?" Kirsten asked.

"Good news. There's room in the supply closet, and we're welcome to put this stuff in there." Adam surveyed their progress. "Looks like you've just about got everything ready. Great work."

Kirsten gestured toward the kids, who stood there with eager expressions. "What else do you need us to do?"

"After you put this stuff in the storage area, you can have the kids come in and help paint signs." Adam let out a harsh breath. "Melody called and said she's not finished at the women's shelter and isn't going to make it after all. This day hasn't exactly turned out like we planned, but we'll make it work."

"We will. We've still got a lot of good workers." Kirsten gave her dad a hug, then smiled at Brady. "And I've got my drill sergeant. He keeps them in line here and in the nursing home."

Adam chuckled. "You two brighten my day. Thanks for the help. I'll show you exactly where to put everything. Follow me."

Brady pointed to Tyler and Zach. "Okay, guys, one of you on each end of the roll."

Tyler and Zach grabbed one roll and marched off behind Adam.

After they put the canopies in the storage area, the group spent the rest of the afternoon painting new booth signs and refurbishing old ones. Brady tried to concentrate on his work, but his attention wandered to Kirsten time after time while she laughed with the children.

The signs finished, Brady walked over to where Kirsten stood. "If you want to drive the kids back to campus, Zach, Tyler and I can stay behind and put away the paint and clean the brushes."

Kirsten nodded. "Good idea. Then I'll come back to get you."

"Okay." Brady turned to the boys as Kirsten left. "You're in charge of putting the lids back on the paint and throwing away the paper in that big trash can over in the corner."

Zach and Tyler wasted no time getting busy with their assignment while Brady washed out the brushes in the sink in the janitor's supply room. Finally, Brady and the boys carefully moved the signs to the storage room. When they finished, he sent the kids off to wash their hands. While Brady made a final check of everything in the storage area, a door squeaked as it opened and closed. Footsteps sounded on the tile floor. Even if he hadn't known Kirsten would return, he would have recognized the sound of her walk. She strode with purpose and determination. He liked that about her, too.

"Brady, where are you?"

"In here." Funny how her voice had annoyed him when he'd listened to her messages. Now it quickened his pulse, and he couldn't hear it often enough. Getting to know the person behind the vexing tones had changed his perspective.

"Ready to go?" She poked her head in the doorway.

"Almost." He reached up to straighten a sign that appeared to be in a precarious position. In the close confines of the storage closet, the sweet, spicy scent of her perfume made him light-headed. "There's—"

"Let me help." She took a step forward and tripped over a box on the floor. She lost her balance. He grabbed her by the shoulders to keep her from falling but didn't manage to catch her until she fell against him.

"You okay?"

Nodding, she steadied herself with her hands splayed across his chest as she gazed into his eyes. "Thanks. Didn't mean to be so clumsy."

Brady swallowed hard, thinking she could be clumsy anytime she wanted when he was around. His pulse pounded in his head. He had to use every ounce of his willpower not to lean over and kiss her. Instead, he practically pushed her away. He flicked off the light as they stepped into the all-purpose room. "Don't worry about it. I never have a problem holding a good-looking woman in my arms."

Turning, she put her hands on her hips. "Can you be serious for more than thirty seconds?"

He'd done it again—hid his feelings behind a flippant remark. He forced himself not to answer right away because he feared whatever he said would sound sarcastic. He counted to ten, then twenty. As he gazed at her, he noticed the little blotch of blue paint on her cheek. Without thinking, he reached over and rubbed his thumb across it. "You have paint on your cheek."

"I do?" Staring at him, she rubbed a hand across the place he'd touched. "Is it gone?"

He nodded. His mind turned to mush, and all he could think about was kissing her. Again.

"Mr. Brady, we're done." Zach charged into the room and stopped abruptly, making Tyler nearly bump into his brother.

Both boys stared at Brady and Kirsten. Brady took a quick step back. He was pretty sure those little boys had a good idea about what they had interrupted. Brady didn't know whether he was thankful for the interruption or not. He smiled at the youngsters. "Would you guys like to grab a burger and head over to the nursing home to meet my gram? She'd love to meet you."

The boys nodded and cheered.

"Am I invited, too?"

"Of course you are. We need a ride." Brady grinned. Things were definitely looking up. Kirsten had invited herself to join them.

"Let's go, then." Kirsten hurried to the van.

After the boys were buckled in to their seat belts, Brady hopped into the passenger seat in the front. "Let's use the drive-through to get our food."

As she started the van, she turned to him with a smile. "Sure. I'll take a cheeseburger. What about Zach and Tyler?"

"Cheeseburgers," they both said.

"Cheeseburgers all around and a cookie for Cora." Brady couldn't help thinking again about the family picture they presented.

The smell of cheeseburgers and fries mingled with the familiar scent of the cleaning fluid used to mop floors in the nursing home. As the nurses' station came into view, Kirsten hoped Jen was away from her desk. If she was there, Brady certainly wouldn't walk by without saying hello. What would she say about the two of them being together with the boys? Kirsten wasn't sure she wanted Jen to know about the upcoming date with Brady. She wouldn't let Kirsten hear the end of it.

"Who's minding the store?" Brady leaned on the work surface.

Jen looked up. "Brady! Kirsten? What are you two doing here on your day off?"

Kirsten resigned herself to the fact that no explanation was going to wipe the speculation off Jen's face. "Visiting Cora. We were doing prep work for the festival."

"That's nice." Jen's smile widened. "Cora had a fantastic time playing cards with her friends, so she might be a little tired."

"We brought her a treat and some company." Brady winked at Jen as if he knew what she was thinking.

"Who are these young men?" Jen winked back.

"Zach and Tyler. They're staying with Adam and me until the children's home where they live gets repaired." Brady tapped the boys on the head as he introduced them. The youngsters charmed Jen almost as if they had been taking lessons from Brady.

As they walked to Cora's room, Kirsten couldn't forget the way Brady had looked at her when she'd stumbled against him in the storage closet. While he'd held her, she thought he was going to kiss her, and then again when he'd wiped the paint off her face. Her imagination was probably working overtime.

But what would she have done if he had? The thought of his kiss tumbled her insides. Brady and all his charm was getting to her.

When they entered Cora's room, she was looking out the window but turned as Brady reached her bedside. She clapped her hands together. "Two of my favorite people. And who do you have with you?"

Once again Brady introduced Zach and Tyler, then leaned over and kissed Cora on the cheek. "I'd better be one of your favorite people."

Cora wagged a finger at him. "You certainly weren't when you took that motorcycle apart in my living room."

Brady shook his head. "Aren't you ever going to forgive me for that?"

"Oh, I've forgiven you, but I certainly haven't forgotten." Cora chuckled as she motioned to Kirsten. "Come over here, and let me give you a hug. The days aren't the same when you aren't here. So glad you stopped by on your day off."

Kirsten sat in the chair Brady motioned her toward and then directed her attention to Cora. "Were you a winner at bridge?"

Cora frowned. "I had terrible cards. Hardly played a hand all afternoon, but I so enjoyed being with my friends."

"That's what counts." Brady held up one of the bags he carried. "I've got a treat for you."

Cora's expression brightened. "What is it?"

He set the bag on the tray table. "Have a look."

Cora peered into the bag, then looked up at Brady, her grin wide as she extracted one of the treats. "Chocolate chip cookies. My favorite. Thank you."

"You're welcome." Brady sat on the bed and opened his own sack as the boys joined him. "We haven't had a chance to eat, so we brought our food with us."

"You're welcome to eat here, but don't get crumbs in my bed." Cora chuckled.

Kirsten took out her burger and unwrapped it as she listened to the banter between Brady and Cora. There was a special bond between them—something Kirsten had never had with her grandparents. Her paternal grandfather had died before she was ever born, and her grandmother had died when she was only three. Her mother's parents had lived on the West Coast, and Kirsten saw them only once or twice a year before they passed away when she was in high school.

She suspected that part of her initial animosity toward Brady stemmed from her mistaken idea that he couldn't be bothered with his ailing grandmother. She'd hated that he was squandering his relationship with his only grandparent while the untimely deaths of her grandparents had robbed her of the opportunity to be close to them. Now he was making up for lost time with Cora and burying all her misjudgments.

"You're awfully quiet." Brady looked at her, concern wrinkling his brow.

Kirsten shrugged, glad he couldn't read her mind. "Just enjoying my food and thinking about how we're going to get everything ready for the festival since we couldn't put the booths up today because of the threat of rain."

"Sure hope they have the extended forecast correct." Brady took a bite of his burger.

"They do." Cora eyed them both. "I can feel the rainy weather coming in my bones."

"Seriously, Gram?"

Cora wagged a finger at Brady. "You can count on it. These old bones can predict the weather."

Brady laughed. "I had no idea."

"Now don't make fun." Cora narrowed her gaze as she looked at Brady. "Show some respect to your elders, young man."

"Yes, ma'am." Standing, Brady saluted. "I think it's time for us to leave, so your old bones can get some rest. You've had a busy day."

"Who says I'm tired?" Cora frowned. "I want to talk with these young men some more."

Brady sighed as he shook his head. "A few more minutes."

Cora looked over at Zach and Tyler. "Do you boys know how to play any card games?"

Zach shrugged, and Tyler shook his head. "Nobody ever taught us."

"Well, Brady will have to bring you by more often, and I can teach you. Would you like that?"

The boys nodded in unison.

"Are you boys going to the festival?" Cora asked.

Again they nodded. Zach hopped off the bed. "It's a lot of fun."

Cora looked over at Kirsten. "Do you suppose they'll let me out of here to go to the festival?"

Kirsten didn't want to make any promises she couldn't keep. "We'll have to check with the doc and therapist, and you know Brady won't be able to take you because he'll be working."

"Yeah, Gram."

Cora lifted her chin in a defiant gesture. "My friends will take me. I don't need a babysitter."

Brady patted Cora's shoulder. "Kirsten will see whether you're allowed to go."

"Okay, but I can hardly wait to get out of this place, so I don't have to check with someone every time I want to step out of my room." Cora pressed her lips together as she eyed Brady and Kirsten.

Kirsten didn't respond, deciding to say nothing rather than get in an argument with Cora. Brady could do the talking. He had a way of winding Cora around his little finger, or maybe it was the other way around. Sure enough, within seconds, Brady had his grandmother smiling again.

He leaned over and kissed Cora's cheek. "Get a good night's rest, and I'll see you tomorrow."

Cora motioned to Zach and Tyler. "You boys deserve a hug, too."

The youngsters shuffled over to Cora, and she gave them each a hug.

When they went by the nurses' station on the way out, Kirsten welcomed the fact that Jen wasn't there. No explanations would be needed until Kirsten came to work on Monday. She wondered what she could say about why she'd been with Brady tonight without Jen having her speculation antennae up in full force. She couldn't reveal the truth to her friend. She didn't even want to admit it to herself. She was beginning to like this man too much for her own good.

Chapter Eight

Brady held open the door as Kirsten and the boys walked out of the nursing home. The security lights atop the tall poles cast long shadows across the quad. Other than a dog barking in the distance, the night was quiet as the foursome walked to the parking lot.

After Kirsten reached her car, she turned. "Guess I'll be heading home. Thanks for your help today."

"You're welcome."

"Mr. Brady." Zach tapped Brady on the arm. "Can Ms. Kirsten come over and watch a movie with us like she did the night of the fire? Please?"

"It's okay with me, but it's up to her." Glancing at Kirsten, Brady wondered what she would say.

Before Kirsten could respond, Tyler ran over and pulled on Kirsten's arm. "You want to come, don't you?"

"I guess this is an offer I can't refuse." Kirsten chuckled.

The boys cheered, and Brady suspected that the two little boys were trying their hands at matchmaking. Did Kirsten suspect as much?

"Will you make popcorn for us again?" Zach opened the back door of Brady's pickup.

Kirsten laughed again. "So that's why you invited me. You want my popcorn."

Brady drank in the sound of her laughter. "You do make the best popcorn I've had since Cora used to make it for me when I was a kid."

"Okay, I'll make popcorn, too. I'll meet you at the house in a few minutes." Kirsten got into her car and started the engine. The headlights illuminated the nearly empty parking lot.

Brady hopped into his pickup and followed her to the gate and out onto the main road. While he drove to Adam's house, the boys tussled in the backseat.

"Don't look at me," Zach hollered.

"You looked at me first," Tyler yelled back.

Brady glanced at the boys in the rearview mirror. "If you guys want a movie and popcorn, you'd better behave."

"He started it," Zach mumbled.

"It doesn't matter who started it. You both need to stop it now, or I'll call Ms. Kirsten and tell her the movie is off."

"Okay." Their barely audible response floated to the front seat.

Watching in the rearview mirror, Brady observed the pouts that formed on the two young faces. He wondered what had brought on the sudden disharmony between the two boys. They'd been well behaved all day until now. Maybe their allotment of goodness had run out. The boys sat in silence for the rest of the trip.

When Brady stopped in the driveway, Zach and Tyler unbuckled their seat belts, hopped out of the car and raced to greet Kirsten, who parked her car behind Brady's. They scrambled to escort her to the door, and Brady breathed a sigh of relief when they didn't erupt into a disagreement or, worse, a fight like they'd had on the drive over.

Kirsten smiled at Brady as they made their way into the house. Despite the boys' bad behavior, Brady was thankful for the two little matchmakers who had extended his time with Kirsten.

Kirsten glanced around. "Looks like my dad isn't home yet."

"Yeah, he said he was going over to Debra's to work on some of the prizes for the booths at the festival." Brady dumped his keys in the dish on the entry table, then turned to Zach and Tyler. "Hey, guys. You get ready for bed, then pick out your movie. I'll help Kirsten with the popcorn."

"Yay!" The boys raced toward the stairs to the lower level.

"And how are you going to help me?" Kirsten raised her eyebrows as she gazed at him.

Brady stepped toward the kitchen. "Get out the bowls. Melt the butter?"

"Okay. That's fine. I just don't want you messing with my technique."

"I wouldn't want to do that." Brady opened a cupboard and brought out the bowls, then went to the refrigerator and got a stick of butter. "How much butter do you want?"

"Half a stick should be good." Kirsten poured some oil into a large skillet and put three kernels of popcorn in it before putting on the lid. Then she turned to look at Brady. "Do you think this thing with my dad and Debra is getting serious? They seem to be spending a lot of time together."

Brady shrugged. "If you want the answer to that, you'll have to ask him."

"He'll think I'm nosy."

"Well, aren't you?"

"Okay, you got me there." Three successive pops accompanied Kirsten's laughter. She picked up the lid and poured in the popcorn. "Are you saying I should mind my own business?"

"I only said if you want to know something, you have to ask." Brady put the butter in the microwave. "I want to ask *you* something. Do you know anything about the circumstances surrounding Zach and Tyler?"

A little frown knit Kirsten's eyebrows as she shook the skillet while the kernels popped. "Why?"

"Other than that first night, they've been pretty well behaved, but tonight on the way here, they started fighting with each other." The microwave beeped and Brady retrieved the cup containing the melted butter.

"It's probably typical sibling rivalry, but we both know that the kids at The Village have come from troubled homes. So maybe their acting out has something to do with that." Kirsten lifted the skillet from the stove as the popping sounds subsided. "You should talk to the Dunns if you want more information about the boys."

"Will they think I'm intruding?" Brady tried to hold back a grin. "I'm actually being serious here. I want things to go smoothly with them."

"You've really grown attached to those boys, haven't you?"

Brady didn't miss the sad look in Kirsten's eyes. Was she thinking about her work with the children in Brazil? "I have, and now that I'm working evenings, I miss helping them with their schoolwork and putting them to bed. I'll definitely miss them when they move back in with the Dunns."

Before Kirsten could respond, the boys charged into

the room. Zach waved a DVD case above his head. "We picked out the movie. *The Incredibles*."

"That's a good one." Brady brought the melted butter to Kirsten.

Tyler stood on his tiptoes as he peered into the bowl Kirsten was filling with popcorn. He snitched a kernel from the top of the pile.

"Hey, you can't have popcorn before it's ready." Zach slammed the DVD case on the kitchen counter.

Brady gave Zach a no-nonsense look. "That wasn't necessary."

Zach frowned but didn't say a thing. Brady hoped there wouldn't be a repeat of the argument in his pickup. He knew what it was like to lose parents, but he didn't know how it was to have a brother, and Kirsten didn't know about having a sibling, either. Why worry about it? He and Kirsten had handled the situation the night of the fire. Tonight they would do the same.

"Brady, why don't you take the boys downstairs and get the movie set up while I put the butter and salt on the popcorn." Kirsten pointed toward the bowls on the counter. "Please take those with you. I'll be down in a minute."

Giving Kirsten a smile, Brady saluted. "Yes, ma'am."

He followed the boys as they raced to the DVD player. Holding the bowls, he held his breath when Zach brought out the DVD and Tyler punched the button to open the player. Cooperation between the boys had Brady releasing a sigh of relief. Hopefully, this would set a tone for the rest of the evening.

"Here you are." The delicious aroma of buttered popcorn filled the room as Kirsten appeared. "Is the movie ready?"

Zach and Tyler nodded and bounded over to get their bowls of popcorn and settle on the sectional. Brady filled his own bowl and Kirsten dimmed the light as he started the movie. Smiling, she settled next to him on the sectional. Her smile made his heart thump against his ribs. Once again, the two of them together with the kids made him think of family. The movie about a superhero family underscored his thoughts. He wanted to be a hero to Kirsten and the two little boys. How could he make that happen?

After the movie was over, Kirsten and Brady listened to the boys' bedtime prayers and tucked them into bed. They said good-night, and Brady followed Kirsten out of the room. As they went up the stairs, he asked, "Do you have a few minutes to talk?"

Kirsten gave him a curious glance. "Sure."

"We can talk while we wash the popcorn bowls." Brady motioned toward the top of the stairs.

When they reached the kitchen, she put the bowls in the sink. "What did you want to talk about?"

"I've decided to take your advice."

"About what?"

"I found an online program where I can get my nursing degree. One where I can start classes in a couple of weeks." Brady held his breath while he waited for Kirsten's response.

"Wow! That's a sudden decision. What brought that about?" Disbelief painted Kirsten's expression. "Are you sure that's what you want to do?"

Slowly releasing his breath, Brady nodded. "Even though I've been at the nursing home for a short time, I've discovered I enjoy working with geriatric patients. That's what I want to do. And this way I'll be here for Cora."

"I know one thing, the patients all love you. So it sounds like you've found your calling." A half smile curved Kirsten's mouth. "Have you told Cora?"

"I told her I was thinking about it, and she's been praying about my decision, and so have your dad and Lovie."

Kirsten's smile broadened. "Now that's a powerful prayer team. No wonder you came to a quick decision."

"I found a program that works with the GI Bill and has flexible starting times. Everything just fell into place—like that's what God had planned for me."

"That's the way things worked for me when I went to Brazil ten years ago, so I understand how you feel."

Brady didn't miss the sadness in Kirsten's eyes. He hated that her inability to return made her unhappy. He wished she could find happiness here—happiness with him. But wasn't he getting way ahead of himself? He needed more time to be sure of his own feelings, and she needed more time to see where God might be leading her—leading them both.

"And I'm also changing shifts. I'm going to begin working days so I can be done when Zach and Tyler are finished with school." Brady wiped the bowls that Kirsten set in the dish rack.

Kirsten shook her head as a little frown knit her eyebrows. "Really?"

"Yeah. I know I just started, but I talked to Ian and Jen about the schedule, and they said it could be worked out."

Laughing, Kirsten continued to shake her head. "I think there are a lot of people trying to push us together."

Was she talking about Zach and Tyler? Brady grinned. "I like that idea, but why do you say that?"

"Because Jen just asked me if I'd start working days because another nurse wants to switch to the later shift. That shift is better for her family situation right now." Kirsten let the water out of the sink.

"Did you agree?"

Kirsten smiled. "I did. Guess we're going to be stuck with each other."

"I like being stuck with you, even if you are sometimes a little bossy." Brady winked.

"I have to be to keep you in line."

Brady laughed. "Did you hear that from Cora?"

Kirsten couldn't hide a smile as she looked at him. "I did."

"Well, she knows me better than anyone, but I want you to be right up there with her. I'm looking forward to that date."

Kirsten just smiled, but even though she didn't say it, Brady was pretty sure she was excited for their date, too. Next weekend was the fall festival, and then they'd have their day out. Time couldn't move fast enough.

Working side by side with Kirsten as they made the last-minute preparations in the festival food booth made Brady even more eager to take her out. A breeze ruffled her hair just then as she stood next to the grill, and he had the urge to reach out and brush the stray tendrils back from her face. He gripped one of the poles holding up the canopy in order to stop himself.

Would it be a step toward convincing her not to go back to Brazil? She wanted to do God's work there. Was his eagerness to change her mind a selfish thought? When he'd first arrived at The Village, he'd made the decision to think less of himself and more of others. Had he come even close to accomplishing that? The questions gathered in his mind like the folks making their way into the festival grounds.

Kirsten had given assignments to her crew and instructions for handling the lunchtime crowd. For now they were mostly selling drinks and snacks. Brady admired her for her organizational skills. She had everything under control.

"Hey, I see your dad's on the schedule to be in the dunking booth. I have to see that." Brady checked the cord on the popcorn cart.

"He does this every year and usually draws quite a crowd. How come you didn't sign up to be in it?" Kirsten helped herself to a bag of popcorn.

Brady tried not to frown. Why did she have to ask that question? Was she trying to get rid of him? "I thought you needed me more than the dunking booth."

Shaking her head, she gave him a silly smile. "I should've known you'd come up with an answer like that."

"Let's leave the dunking booth to brave men like your dad. Nobody knows me, but your dad is well-known and can entice a lot of people to plunk down their money so they can see him go into the tank."

Kirsten nodded again, a little mist forming in her eyes as she gazed up at him. "My mom was the brave one. The last year she was with us, she didn't have the strength to throw the ball, but she was determined to dunk my dad as she'd done every year since they started the festival. I teamed up with her and helped her reach that goal. It's hard being without her this year."

"I'm sure your dad's remembering her, too." Brady stood there, resisting the urge to put his arms around Kirsten and console her. "How do you think your dad's doing?"

"I think it's a good sign that he's seeing a lot of Debra. It shows me he's moving on with his life." Kirsten filled the napkin holder and handed a package of napkins to one of the other helpers before turning back to him. "You should have a pretty good read on that since you're living there."

Brady busied himself with a container of drinks. "I wish I could say I did, but your dad keeps to himself a lot. I'm a little concerned I'm invading his space even though he's the one who suggested I rent a room from him. I'm glad when you come over for dinner because he seems more alive when you're there. I've noticed how much he enjoys your visits."

"Are you saying I shouldn't have moved out?"

Brady's mind buzzed with her question. Had he made a misstep again? He thought he'd given her a compliment, but instead it seemed he'd made her feel guilty. "No, you need your own life as much as your dad needs his."

"Thanks for that reassurance." Kirsten refilled the napkin holder on the counter. "What about Zach and Tyler? Does he interact with them?"

"Yeah, I didn't mean to make it sound like he never interacts with us. He just keeps to himself after the boys go to bed, and I wonder if I'm getting in his way... overstaying my welcome."

"Don't read my dad's quietness as a sign he doesn't want you around." Kirsten continued to ready the supplies. "He's always been a rather introspective person. Mom and I were the talkers."

"That's good to know."

"I'm sure he appreciates your help with Zach and Tyler. He said they can be a handful."

Brady chuckled. "They're boys. They're loud and rambunctious—probably very different than the little girl he raised."

"Is that what he told you?"

"Not exactly, but I guessed as much from his comments when Zach and Tyler were chasing each other through the house." Brady laughed again. "They kind of remind me of the way I was when I was a youngster. Though I didn't have a brother, Cora would tell you I was a handful all by myself."

"I suppose that helps you relate to those boys." Kirsten's brow knit in little frown. "Did you find out why they came to live at The Village?"

Brady shook his head as he lit another grill. "I haven't spoken with the Dunns. I intend to do so when I get a chance. I didn't want to ask the boys directly because I wasn't sure they'd want to say anything about it. I know I didn't want to talk about what happened with my family."

"Do you think that was a good thing? Never confiding in anyone?"

Brady didn't know how to answer that. Would his life have taken a different course if he'd been more open about his feelings? Somehow he doubted that. He'd made a lot of rash decisions in his life—leaving his grandmother's house in anger, not finishing high school and jumping from job to job. He hoped he could take a more measured approach with his choices in the future and be less reticent about sharing his thoughts. "Good question. Wish I had an answer. One thing I do know. Turning my life over to God made a big difference in the way I look at things."

"I know what you mean. Though I have to admit that leaving the decision about Brazil in God's hands isn't easy. I want to go back so badly."

What could he say? He wasn't in her corner when it came to her wish to return to the mission field. "We could get that super prayer team involved."

Kirsten gave him a sad little smile. "I'm afraid at least a third of that team doesn't want me to go back."

"You mean your dad?"

"Yeah."

"I can understand where he's coming from. He'd like to have his only child nearby."

Kirsten sighed. "That's what Jen says, too."

"There are a whole lot of people who don't want to see you go. Me included." There. He'd said it. Would it make a difference to her?

She stared at him, a question in her eyes. "So you'd be happy to keep me around?"

Brady gazed back. Did her look mean she wasn't sure what to think of his statement? He'd told her how he felt about her leaving, but maybe he should keep things light for now. "Yeah, I want to keep you around. After all, who will keep me in line if you're not here?"

"Cora."

Brady laughed. "True, but she needs your help, too."

"She's doing pretty well on her own." Kirsten put more drinks in a nearby cooler. "She's really proud of you, and she's so happy you're using your medical skills at the nursing home. You're an asset to our team."

Brady basked in Kirsten's approval. "Thanks. I wasn't sure how this job was going to work out because of my experiences on the battlefield. Medicine there can be hard on the psyche. A lot of medics suffer from PTSD right along with those soldiers who are wounded in combat. We had to look out for that in our patients and in ourselves."

Kirsten shook her head. "I can't imagine what you had to deal with as an army medic."

Brady didn't want to talk about that time. He'd seen too many gruesome things. Hoping to change the subject, he leaned closer to Kirsten. "I have something I'd like to discuss with you. We can talk later when the rush is over."

"Why can't you do it now?"

He let a lazy smile spread across his face. "I didn't know you were so impatient."

"I'm not impatient."

"Then you can wait. I want your full attention when we talk—no customers to distract you. Besides, I have burgers to flip." Giving her a wink, Brady twirled the flipper like a baton and returned to the grill.

His conversation with Kirsten had him eager for their date. He wanted to get to know this fascinating woman even more than before. She loved her dad, and the loss of her mom had obviously brought Kirsten a lot of sorrow. Was that why she often appeared to be all business? He hoped he could help her learn to laugh—to have fun. He hoped he wasn't expecting too much.

Chapter Nine

Kirsten watched folks of every age gather in front of the different festival booths to have their faces painted, or buy a grab bag or play a game. There were two bouncy houses and an inflatable slide for the kids, as well as pony rides. The baked goods sale and live auction attracted the adults. There was something for everyone. The festival was in full swing.

Trying to concentrate on customers rather than her earlier conversation with Brady, Kirsten took in the laughter and jovial voices swirling through the church parking lot. But Brady was a hard man to ignore. Being with him was like being in one of the bouncy houses. She didn't know what would happen next, but she wanted to go along for the fun.

Kirsten let out a sigh as she handed two hot dogs to a young man, who then smothered them in mustard. She continued to fill orders and tried not to think about what was on Brady's mind. Was it something good or something bad? Did it have to do with Cora? Or maybe her dad? All these questions had her thoughts in a muddle.

After the lunchtime rush was over, Kirsten breathed a sigh of relief as she glanced over her crew. "Thanks, everyone, we've made it through the busiest part of the day. You made it all possible."

"There's someone here who deserves a round of applause." Brady came over and waved a hand above her head. "Let's hear it for Kirsten."

A loud cheer arose in the booth accompanied by utensils banging against metal pots. Kirsten turned to Brady with an indulgent smile. "Thank you, but this is a team effort."

"But you're our director." Brady nodded as he looked over the group. "You keep us in line."

"I'm glad I have you all fooled." Kirsten laughed as a collective chuckle rose from the group. "Okay, since our big rush is over, I'm going to give each of you a break, two at a time so you can take in some of the festival."

Minutes later, Brady sauntered over to where she was organizing plates, cups and napkins. "Should I turn off the grills?"

Kirsten shook her head. "Keep one going. You can turn the others off. We'll probably have a few requests for burgers or hot dogs, but not that many for the rest of the afternoon."

"Okay, fearless leader." Brady saluted.

Kirsten let out an exasperated sigh. "I'm not your fearless leader."

Brady raised his eyebrows. "You're not?"

"Quit teasing."

"But it's so much fun."

"For you." Kirsten shook her head, wondering if this was a good time to ask him about his earlier wish to talk to her. "Things have quieted down. What did you want to talk about?"

Brady glanced around the booth, then stepped closer. "I'll tell you if you step into my office."

"Your office?"

"Yeah, right over here." Brady motioned to a spot on the other side of the grills at the back of the booth.

Kirsten narrowed her gaze as she followed him. "What's this about?"

"Our date."

"What about it?"

"You said we'd have our date after the festival, so I'm ready to set a time."

"But I don't have the schedule, and technically you weren't supposed to mention it until the festival is over."

"But it's almost over, and I have the schedule."

Kirsten wasn't even going to ask how he already had the schedule for the upcoming weeks. Jen had given it to him. She was pushing them together at every opportunity—like Cora and even like her dad. "So do we have the same day off this coming week?"

"Friday."

"I'm not surprised Jen scheduled it that way."

"You're saying Jen purposely gave us the same day off?" Brady gave Kirsten a curious look.

Kirsten nodded. "She's been trying to get me to go out with you from the moment you showed up at the nurses' station."

"Then we shouldn't disappoint her."

Kirsten wasn't sure how to respond to that statement. What was he planning? She wasn't even sure she wanted Jen to know about the date. What if the date went badly? Was it wise to date a coworker? Why hadn't she asked herself these questions before agreeing to go out with him? "What time on Friday?"

"I'll have to call you after I make the plans. This is going to be one big surprise." He grinned.

Kirsten wasn't sure she liked surprises. "Don't make it too big."

"It'll be just right." He waggled his eyebrows.

"Like the story of Goldilocks?"

Nodding, Brady chuckled. "Exactly, except there will be no big bad bears or even little ones."

"You're sure?" Kirsten tried not to smile at his silly joke.

"Absolutely. Now back to work."

Kirsten nodded and sent two more of her workers off to experience the festival. While she tried to push thoughts of this date to the back of her mind, Cora and her friends Liz and Ruby stopped by for some refreshments. Kirsten leaned on the counter. "Are you ladies enjoying the festival?"

Cora glanced back at her friends. "Yes, they've been pushing me around in my chariot. Wish I could maneuver on my own, but I'm just happy to be out and about."

"Gram, you've got some good friends." Brady looked at Liz and Ruby. "Thanks for bringing her out."

Ruby nodded. "We're showing her a good time."

"I'm showing *them* a good time." Cora laughed as she patted one cheek and turned her face. "What do you think of my face painting?"

Brady joined Kirsten and peered over the counter at his grandmother. "Gram, you look fantastic with that pumpkin painted on your face."

"Now don't you make fun of your old gram."

Brady looked at Kirsten. "Didn't I just tell her that she looked fantastic? Is that making fun?"

Kirsten shrugged as she produced an innocent look. "Maybe your joking has finally caught up to you."

Cora laughed. "I know he likes to tease, so I thought I'd give him a little of his own medicine."

Kirsten joined in the laughter. Was that what she needed to do—give Brady some of his own medicine? Had God brought Brady into her life to help her find a little more laughter? She kept asking herself what God's plan was, but she didn't know how to deal with Brady and his part in her life. Her wish to return to mission work served as a big blockade when it came to a relationship with Brady, but even if that wasn't an issue, her inability to have children flashed through her mind like a big warning sign. She'd suffered that hurt once before. She didn't want to be disappointed again. *Have fun*, she told herself. *Enjoy his attention. Keep it light.*

"Where are Zach and Tyler today?" Cora asked as she looked around.

"The boys are hanging out with the Dunns, their house parents."

Cora pressed her lips together in a frown. "I was hoping to take those boys to some of the booths, especially the dunking booth."

"If you're going to try to dunk my dad, you should head that way now." Kirsten looked over at Brady. "You want to take your break now?"

"You have to come, too." Cora spoke up before Brady could answer.

"I think that's an excellent idea." Brady gave her a knowing smile.

"We have to make sure we have enough people taking care of the booth." Kirsten glanced around.

Brady waved his hand toward the four college-age young people who stood near the counter as they talked. "Looks like you have a group that can handle things while you're gone."

Kirsten couldn't argue with him. "Okay, let's see who can dunk my dad."

"Does that mean me?" Brady sidled up beside Kirsten.

"It means anyone who buys a ticket."

Unable to contain a grin, Brady looked down at her. "Are you going to cheer for me?"

She looked at him as if he'd asked her to do something illegal. "You expect me to cheer against my dad?"

"You said you wanted to see who could dunk him." Brady raised his eyebrows.

"That doesn't mean I'm going to cheer for you."

"Will you cheer for me?" Cora waved a hand as Liz pushed the wheelchair across the festival grounds.

"Okay, I'll cheer for everyone." Kirsten held out her hands in a sign of surrender. "My poor dad. Even his daughter won't be on his side."

Kirsten couldn't help remembering last year when she'd helped her mom dunk her dad, but this was different. A lump of sadness lodged in her throat. If only her mom was here to join in the fun *and* give her advice about Brady. What would her mom have to say? Kirsten wished she knew.

A large crowd was gathered around the dunking booth as Brady and Kirsten approached. Adam sat on the seat inside. A loud cheer went up when a ball hit the target, but a collective groan filled the air when it failed to trigger the mechanism that would send Adam into the water.

"Better get in line. It's already long." Kirsten gave Brady a no-nonsense look.

He looked down at his grandmother as she fished in her purse and produced a ticket. "I'm ready. Let's get in line."

Brady grabbed hold of the handles on Cora's wheelchair as he grinned at Kirsten. "We're off."

Adam sparred with the folks who attempted to put him

in the water. The number of spectators grew as Lovie tried her hand at bringing down her boss. When Lovie's last try failed, the crowd gave her a rousing cheer and urged her to try again. Wagging a finger at Adam, she marched over and purchased another ticket and got back in line.

Brady smiled over at Kirsten as he and Cora drew closer and closer to the front. She smiled back as if to say he wouldn't find success. When Cora's turn came, Brady offered his help, but his grandmother would have none of it. She wanted to do this on her own.

The crowd chanted Cora's name as she gave it her all, but none of her three balls hit the target. She looked up at Brady. "Should I give it another try like Lovie?"

Brady shrugged. "That's up to you, Gram."

Cora shook her head and turned her head toward Adam. "You're lucky I'm not in my best form. You wait till next year."

Adam laughed. "I'll be ready."

"My grandson will show you how it's done." Cora looked over at Brady. "Send him into the water."

"Okay, Gram. This is for you and me both." Brady stepped to the line.

He took the ball from the booth operator. What if he failed? He'd look like a fool, and Kirsten would get the last laugh. She wouldn't let him live it down.

He shook the negative thought away. He had to get over himself. This was about having some fun for a good cause, whether he dunked Adam or not. Taking a deep breath, Brady fingered the sphere. He'd never been much of a baseball player. Soccer had been his sport. Too bad he couldn't kick a soccer ball into the target.

When he stepped up to the mark, he glanced at Kirsten. She was watching him with a smug expression.

Then he looked up at Adam, who had the same look on his face. "Ready to go down?"

"I'm safe. You can't hit the broad side of a barn." Adam leaned back and crossed his arms as the folks in the crowd chuckled.

"A little overconfident, don't you think?"

"Show me what you've got."

Brady wound up his arm in an exaggerated motion. "Got my throwing arm in great condition from flipping burgers."

"That's all you can do—flip burgers." Adam guffawed.

With his heart pounding, Brady didn't dare look at Kirsten. He wound up like a baseball pitcher and let the ball fly. When it hit the tarp behind the target with a thud and didn't even graze the metal piece, Brady's confidence took a nosedive. He definitely wasn't going to look in the pretty nurse's direction now.

Brady waved a hand at Adam. "I was warming up the arm. You're going down this time."

"Give it your best shot."

Brady took aim. This time he wouldn't throw so hard. He lobbed the ball toward the target. The ball clanged against the metal, but he hadn't thrown it hard enough to trigger the mechanism. After the crowded finished lamenting, they cheered him on as the attendant gave him the last ball. He had to make a throw somewhere between the first one and the second one. Harder, but not too hard.

Stepping up to the line again, Brady breathed deeply. He brought his arm back and heaved the ball. When it hit the target, a sound reverberated through the air. Nothing happened. He'd hit the target hard. Why didn't Adam go down?

As Brady turned away in defeat, the seat collapsed in

a delayed reaction. Adam plunged into the water, making a huge splash. The crowd went wild, and Brady looked over at Kirsten with a triumphant grin. She looked back at him with a barely perceptible smile.

"Mr. Brady, Mr. Brady, you dunked Mr. Adam." Zach came running out of the crowd with Tyler following close behind. "That was so cool."

Brady tousled the boys' hair while he relished their admiration. "Mr. Adam almost didn't go down."

"That was the exciting part." Tyler's eyes were wide with excitement. "Is it okay if we hang out with you now?"

Before Brady could reply, Tony Dunn emerged through the throng. "Zach and Tyler, what did we say about staying with us?"

The boys jerked their heads toward Tony, their eyes wide with panic. Tyler stepped behind Zach as he backed up. The two youngsters collided and hung their heads, not saying a word.

Not wanting the boys to get into trouble, Brady quickly stepped in and put his hands on their shoulders and looked down at their frightened faces. "Mr. Tony made that rule for your protection, and you didn't obey. Do you have something you'd like to say to Mr. Tony?"

"Sorry." The boys mumbled the word in unison.

Tony came over and hunkered down next to the kids. "Hey, guys, I'm not angry with you. I just wanted you to remember how important it is to stay with the people who are in charge. And today that means Ms. Rebecca and me. We don't want anything to happen to you, so we want to make sure we know where you are at all times. Do you understand?"

Still silent, Zach and Tyler nodded, their little faces sorrowful. Zach finally looked up. "Yes, sir."

"Do you have some time to talk privately?" Brady eyed Tony, then glanced over at Kirsten. "Can you spare me for a few more minutes while I talk to Tony?"

"Sure." Kirsten nodded.

Tyler tugged on Brady's arm. "Can we stay with Ms. Kirsten?"

When they looked up at the two men for confirmation, Kirsten stepped forward. "It's fine if Zach and Tyler come with me. We'll go with Cora. She wanted to take the boys to some of the booths."

"What do you say?" Brady looked at Tony.

Tony gave the boys a solemn look. "You must stay with Ms. Kirsten at all times. No running off for any reason."

Zach and Tyler nodded.

"Call me if they need me," Brady said.

"I will," Kirsten told him as she ushered Zach and Tyler toward Cora, who sat nearby in her wheelchair.

Tony gave Brady a sideways glance while they walked toward the food booth. "I'm glad you asked to talk. I wanted to tell you some things about Zach and Tyler."

Brady smiled. "That's exactly why I wanted a moment. What information can you give me about them?"

"First, I want to tell you how much they love staying with you and Adam."

"They're a handful, but we're enjoying the experience."

Tony nodded. "They can be a challenge. They look up to you, so that helps. They haven't stopped talking about you all day."

Tony's statement made Brady realize more than ever that he had to be a good example for Zach and Tyler. That was becoming more evident every day. He would never have dreamed that someday someone would be looking up to him. "Guess I'd better be on my best behavior."

"Yeah, it's a big responsibility, and that brings me to the point I wanted to make with you. We get calls for kids to come live at The Village, and we don't always have room." Tony looked Brady right in the eye. "Would you be interested in applying to be a foster parent, so you could take care of Zach and Tyler more permanently?"

Brady didn't know what to say. Was this something he wanted to do? "Can a single person be a foster parent?"

"Absolutely. Adam is one, so the boys could stay there with no problem, but I thought you might like to be official, as well."

Brady slowly nodded. "Yeah, I'd like to do that."

"Super! That way Rebecca and I can take in two more children when we get back in the house." Tony clapped Brady on the back. "We are working with DFCS to make all this happen. I've already mentioned this to Adam, and he told me to ask you. So he's on board with having Zach and Tyler full-time."

"When do you plan to tell the boys about this new arrangement?"

"When we know that you've been approved. First, you'll have to go through an intensive weekend training session and pass all the screening and background checks."

"Just let me know where and when. Are Zach and Tyler eligible for adoption?"

Tony nodded. "Because of abuse, their parents lost parental rights when the boys were just four and five. They went to live with their grandparents at that time, but their grandmother got cancer and died a year later and the grandfather's health deteriorated until he couldn't take care of the boys anymore. That's when they came to live at The Village. They've been part of our family group for three years. Their grandfather also died at the beginning of the year."

"Are they without any family?"

"An aunt and uncle, but they've showed no interest in taking the boys." Tony's brow wrinkled. "I want you to understand what they went through before they lived with their grandparents."

"Was the abuse bad?" Brady couldn't relate to that. His parents hadn't been abusive, just distant.

"It was." Tony nodded again. "Did you notice how fearful they were when I came to get them?"

"Yeah."

"I had to be very calm. Even then you could see the fear in their eyes." Tony narrowed his gaze as he shook his head. "They haven't forgotten the beatings, the starvation or being locked in their rooms."

"That must be the reason they never want the bedroom door shut."

Tony nodded. "You must be doing something right because I've always felt it was a delicate balancing act to discipline them without causing them to be fearful."

"Thanks for sharing all this with me. You've answered all the questions I've been wanting to ask." Brady's mind was overwhelmed with the information.

Tony looked back toward the dunking tank. "I'd better get back to Rebecca. I'll let her know that you and Kirsten have Zach and Tyler."

"Thanks." Brady let this conversation soak in. Who would have ever guessed that one day he would be a foster parent? That was just one step away from adoption. The idea settled in his heart. A wild thought for sure.

Kirsten watched Zach and Tyler skip alongside Cora's wheelchair as Ruby pushed it toward the food booth. Cora had taken those little boys under her wing as surely as she'd taken Brady in when he'd been about that age. As they drew closer to the booth, Kirsten saw her dad talking with Brady as he served a customer a drink and a hot dog.

Everything was under control. Everything except her heart. The most unlikely man was beginning to find a place there, and she wasn't sure she should let it happen. They hadn't even gone on their first date yet and he was already consuming her thoughts. She kept wondering whether she should tell her dad about the date. She had always shared things with him, but she was afraid he would see the prospect of this relationship as a way to keep her in Georgia.

Would Brady mention it to her dad? So far it appeared that he hadn't said a thing. What did that mean?

Brady glanced up and smiled. "Could I interest you folks in some of our delicious food?"

Cora chortled as Ruby brought the wheelchair to a stop. "You remind me of this kid I used to know who had a lemonade stand one summer and practically dragged people off the street to buy his sweet drink," she said, giving him a knowing look.

"I'd forgotten about that." Brady let out a halfhearted laugh. "Did you have to tell everyone?"

Kirsten took in the lighthearted exchange between Cora and Brady. Their interaction always warmed her heart. Kirsten was looking forward to her date with Brady, but she wasn't sure it was a wise thing to let him know. Every time she thought of letting a relationship get serious, she remembered the way Will had looked at her when she'd told him she couldn't have kids. Even all these years later, her heart shriveled at the memory.

Kirsten helped Brady take the group's snack orders. When they finished eating, Cora asked Brady if the boys could go back to the nursing home with her so she could teach them to play cards. After consulting with Adam, Brady gave her the go-ahead.

Before the boys left, Kirsten listened as Brady took them aside. "Okay, guys, Mr. Adam and I are giving you permission to go with Cora. I expect you to be on your best behavior and listen to her and do what she says."

Zach and Tyler nodded their little heads, their expressions serious.

"I want you to remember that she's my gram and very important to me, so I expect you to treat her well."

Tyler contorted his face as he stared at Brady. "Does that mean we have to let her win at cards?"

Brady pressed his lips together, obviously trying to force back laughter. Finally, he cleared his throat. "No, that means you're polite and obedient. When I'm done here, I'll pick you up."

"Can Ms. Kirsten come with you?" Zach asked.

Brady looked over at her. "What do you think?"

Kirsten wasn't surprised that the kids were trying to push Brady and her together. "I can't make any promises. It all depends on how much time it takes to close up the booth."

"Aw." Tyler pouted.

"Are these young men ready to go?" Cora pointed to the street. "The van is ready to take us back."

The boys nodded.

"Okay. Let's head out." Cora waved a hand like she was rallying her troops.

"Remember what I told you," Brady called after the kids.

They nodded and waved as they helped push Cora's wheelchair toward their waiting vehicle.

Brady let out a long, slow breath as he looked at Kirsten. "I hope that wasn't a mistake."

"They'll have fun together." Kirsten smiled at him. "It'll be good for all of them."

"I hope you're right." Brady took a wire brush to one of the grills, anticipating the end of the festival and the closing of the booth.

"I am." Kirsten checked supplies, happy that she had made a good estimate when she'd ordered things way back in the spring. She wished she had that much forethought when it came to the handsome man at her side. Two little boys were crusading to make a match between her and Brady. She couldn't deny how much that appealed to her, but there were too many complications ready to sabotage that match.

The crowd dwindled, and Kirsten had the remaining workers begin to box up the supplies, leaving only the bare necessities for any remaining orders. When the sun sat low in the sky above the tall pines surrounding the parking lot, the booths shut down. Workers scrambled to gather the leftover prizes and break down their booths.

Brady took charge of labeling the parts and stowing them in the cargo van for transport and storage back at The Village. With all the volunteers, the work went quickly. In short order the church parking lot was cleared of booths and trash.

As the last rays of sunlight filtered through the pines, Brady walked over to Kirsten. "Are you going to come with me? I'm pretty sure Zach and Tyler are hoping for a movie and popcorn."

"You're just inviting me because you like my popcorn." Kirsten tried to keep a straight face.

Brady snapped his fingers. "You found me out."

Kirsten laughed. "Yes, and even though you are only using me to get my superior popcorn, I'll go with you."

"A good thing for us all." Brady put an arm around Kirsten's shoulders and escorted her to where their vehicles were parked.

Kirsten's pulse raced, and she tried to keep her equilibrium. So much about today had served to cement her growing interest in Brady, but the thought of a relationship with him scared her—made her doubt her own good sense. A tornado of thoughts whirled in her mind while she followed Brady on the drive back to The Village. Her head told her to run the other way, but her crazy heart told her to embrace the experience. Was her heart looking to get crushed again?

Minutes later when they arrived at Cora's room, a boisterous game of crazy eights was in full swing. Kirsten and Brady stood in the hallway out of sight until the game finished.

Tyler raised his hands in triumph. "I won again!"

Zach grabbed the cards. "Let's play another game, so I can win."

Brady stepped into the room. "Sorry, guys, cards are over for the day."

"Aww." Zach frowned, but politely set the cards on the table.

Cora pushed herself out of her chair and grabbed hold of her walker. "They were great students and formidable opponents. We had a fabulous time. Thanks for letting them come."

"What do you boys say to Ms. Cora?" Brady raised his eyebrows while he looked at the youngsters.

"Thank you," they said together.

"Thanks, Gram, for showing them a good time." Brady leaned over and kissed Cora on the cheek, then propelled the boys toward the hallway with Kirsten following close behind.

Cora pushed her walker toward the door. "Ruby and I took them over to the senior center for dinner, so they've been fed."

Brady turned. "Thanks for that, too."

"Bye, Ms. Cora." Tyler and Zach waved.

"They were very well behaved. You can bring them over anytime." Cora grinned.

After they had gone a little ways down the hall, Tyler stopped and ran back to Cora and gave her a hug. As she hugged him back, Zach joined them. Kirsten's eyes misted as she took in the scene. Every kid needed a grandmother, and every elderly person needed a kid to brighten the day. Kirsten looked over at Brady. He had a faraway look in his eyes. Was he remembering his childhood and hugs from Cora?

After the hugs, the boys ran back down the hallway. The foursome walked out of the nursing home into the cool night air. Zach and Tyler talked nonstop until they arrived at home. Once inside, Brady instructed them to get ready for bed, and they wasted no time racing down the stairs to their bedroom.

Kirsten came up beside Brady. "Do they ever run out of energy?"

"They usually go until they drop." Brady turned to her with a smile. "It's already kind of late for these guys. What do you say we forget the popcorn and movie and play a board game?"

"So you got me over here on false pretenses?"

"Absolutely. I had to think of something." He grinned. "Let's go downstairs to make sure those kids are actually getting ready for bed."

Kirsten followed Brady down the stairs. He disappeared into the bedroom, and Kirsten glanced around the room. She noticed a guitar sitting in a stand at the far end of the sectional.

When Brady returned, she motioned toward the guitar. "Yours?"

"Yeah."

"I didn't know you played guitar."

Brady shrugged. "I mess around with it. I was showing Zach and Tyler a few chords the other night."

"Have you ever thought about playing in the praise band at church?"

Brady shook his head. "Looks like you have enough guitarists in the group."

"We do, but John is looking for someone to take his place. You should come join us at our next practice on Wednesday night."

"Are you sure?"

"Yes. Otherwise, I wouldn't have asked."

"Okay." Brady smiled. "I'll check with your dad to make sure he'll be here for the boys, and if everything's good with him, I'll be there."

"You'll enjoy it. It's a good group."

Zach and Tyler raced out of the bedroom. "Is it movie time?"

"No movie tonight. It's already late, but Ms. Kirsten has agreed to play one game of Sorry! with us."

Kirsten held her breath as she waited for the kids' reaction, but they agreed without a fuss. They even got the game out and set it up on the coffee table. They alternately laughed and moaned and cheered as they moved their playing pieces around the board until Brady won.

"All right. It's time for you guys to go to bed."

Zach protested, but followed his little brother into the bedroom. Kirsten watched while Brady read a chapter from *A Wrinkle in Time*, a book she remembered from her elementary school days. She listened to the familiar story with a growing admiration for the man who took time to read to his charges.

When Brady finished, the boys begged for another, but he reminded them of their deal for one chapter each night. Kirsten smiled at her own memories of her mother reading books at bedtime. Prayers, hugs and good-nights followed. Brady shut off the light and escorted Kirsten back up.

At the top of the stairs, she turned. "When did you start reading to them?"

"One day last week we stopped at the library on campus. The lady who works there was a mountain of information. She helped the boys pick out the books."

"Those boys adore you."

"And I'm getting quite attached to them." Brady took a deep breath. "I had a talk with Tony today, and he asked me to go through the training to become a foster parent. I said I would."

"So what does that mean?" Kirsten let this information roll through her brain. Brady was a man full of surprises.

Brady recounted his conversation with Tony. "It will mean a big responsibility, but it's something I want to do. Cora will be so excited when she finds out."

Nodding, Kirsten smiled, resisting the urge to hug him. "And so will those little boys. I'm excited for you, too. You and Dad are going to have your hands full."

"I know, but I'm ready for the challenge."

"I'd say you are." Kirsten had a challenge of her own. She was losing the battle to keep her heart safe from this charming man. Did his willingness to be a foster parent mean he'd be willing to share life with a woman who couldn't have children? Should she embrace a relationship with him? The thought scared her but not enough to make her back away.

Chapter Ten

With his guitar case in hand, Brady stood at the entrance to the chapel and listened to the music coming from inside. He'd never played with a church group before, but he wanted to be a part of this because Kirsten had invited him. Maybe his motives weren't all noble, but besides being a foster parent, this would be one more way he could show her that he was a good guy. And this was one more chance to find a place to belong.

Brady stepped inside. For a few moments, the dim light in the chapel made it difficult to see, but he could hear people tuning their instruments. As he walked up the aisle, his eyes adjusted and he spied Kirsten talking with a short bearded man holding a guitar. When she saw him, she smiled and stepped off the stage.

"Hey, Brady, thanks for coming." Kirsten motioned to the others in the band. "Everyone, I want you to meet Brady Hewitt."

Brady waved as the rest of the band greeted him. He hoped this venture wasn't a mistake and tried to show the confidence he wasn't feeling. "Kirsten said you could use another guitarist."

"Absolutely." John, the pastor of the Chapel Church,

hopped up on the stage. "Let me introduce you to the others. Mike plays bass guitar. Luke is on keyboards and Leslie on the drums. Kirsten and Phil do vocals."

Mike handed Brady some sheet music as he plugged in his guitar. "Now that you've met everyone, we can get started."

Brady studied the music. He didn't recognize most of it. Although he'd become a Christian several years ago, his church attendance had been sporadic because of his jobs. These were definitely not the hymns he'd heard at the church Cora had attended when he was a kid. He hoped he wouldn't make a mess of things. From the looks of this music, hours of practice lay ahead of him.

Phil picked out the first song, and Brady managed to get through the intro without any major mistakes. That boded well for the rest of the practice. He had his mind totally focused on the music until Kirsten started to sing. The pure tones of her voice drew his attention and made him stumble over a chord. He took a deep breath and refocused his attention. He couldn't let her distract him.

By the time they got to the third song, his confidence had returned. The tension drained from his shoulders, and his fingers found the right chords with ease.

After they finished working on the third song, Phil looked over at Brady. "Do you ever do vocals while you play?"

Brady wondered whether he was going to have to sing. "Sometimes, but I need to concentrate on playing today. I haven't played much in the last year, especially in front of people."

"Hey, you're doing great. I hope we can use you on vocals sometimes." Phil shifted some music on the stand. "We like to switch lead singers."

"Sure. Let me get a little more comfortable with this music before I try singing." Brady nodded.

When they finished, Mike looked Brady's way. "Great practice. Glad you're part of the team."

"Thanks." Brady picked up the music from the stand. "Okay if I take this with me so I can practice more?"

"Sure." Mike waved his hand in the direction of the entrance to The Village. "We usually head over to that dessert and coffee shop down the road. Please join us."

"I'd love to." Brady wondered whether Kirsten intended to go.

Mike nodded. "Meet you there."

"Sure thing." Brady looked toward the spot where Kirsten had been talking on her phone. She wasn't there.

He glanced around the chapel and saw her rushing down the aisle. She slipped out the door before he'd made up his mind to go after her. He put away his guitar and hoped she would be there. If she showed, that would make his night. If she didn't, this would still be an opportunity to get to know some other people near his age. He'd spent most of his time in the past few weeks with Cora, Adam Bailey or two rambunctious boys. Brady was ready to socialize with people who were his contemporaries.

When Brady arrived at the coffee shop, Phil, Mike, Luke and Leslie had already found a table. They waved Brady over. There was no sign of Kirsten. He tried not to be disappointed. With the smell of coffee and chocolate permeating the air around him, Brady grabbed a chair and sat down.

Phil's phone rang, and he answered it. After he ended the phone call, he looked around the table. "Kirsten said to order for her. She'll be here in about ten minutes."

"Let's order." Luke stood.

The others followed Luke to the counter. Brady brought up the rear. While he stood in line, he cast surreptitious glances toward the door, but there was no sign of Kirsten. Why was he twisting himself in knots over a woman he wasn't even sure suited him? For some crazy reason she fascinated him, challenged him and pulled him in as if he had no will to resist her. No other woman had ever made him feel this way. For some inexplicable reason he wanted to win her heart. That was the bottom line. Wasn't that why he'd cajoled her into a date?

After they returned to the table, Phil leaned back and laced his fingers behind his head. "Brady, thanks for joining us. Tell us a little about yourself."

Brady wasn't sure what he wanted to say about his life. He figured he should start with his reason for being here. He told them about Cora, his time in the army, working in the oil fields and on fishing boats, and his newest adventures as an aide in the nursing home and his plans to become a foster parent. They seemed impressed, but he didn't think his life amounted to much.

Just as he finished talking, a waitress brought their orders. Luke offered a short prayer. When the prayer was over, Kirsten walked in the door. The sight of her strummed across Brady's heart. She created a melody that drew him like a siren's song.

"Got your order." Mike shoved a cup in Kirsten's direction as she took the empty seat next to Brady.

"Thanks." Kirsten opened her purse. "What do I owe you?"

"Nothing. My treat." Brady smiled, glad the others had left the empty seat next to him.

She gave him a knowing smile. "You're determined to keep me in your debt, aren't you?"

"No, I'm just paying you back for your help with Cora." Brady took a gulp of his coffee.

"I was just doing my job."

Brady shook his head. "I don't consider helping me pick out a dress for Cora to wear to the wedding part of your job."

Mike slowly nodded his head. "Now I know why you seemed familiar. You were the guy helping the older lady with the walker at Ian's wedding."

Brady nodded. "Yeah."

"So that's Cora. I should've realized when you were talking about her."

"She's one of kind," Kirsten added. "She keeps us on our toes at the nursing home."

Brady looked over the group. "Since you know about me now, I'd like to get to know y'all. How did you get connected with the Chapel Church?"

The four looked at each other as if they weren't sure who should go first. Leslie, who'd been the quietest, raised her hand a few inches. "I'm a college sophomore. John Franklin's my dad. In high school, I started playing with the group. We've had members come and go, but the five of us have been together since Kirsten started singing with us."

Brady would have guessed that Leslie, who was tall and thin like her dad, was older. "Are you sure your dad doesn't mind my taking his place?"

Leslie nodded. "He's super glad you want to be part of the band. It frees up another night for him."

Mike set his drink on the table. "Guess I'll go next. Us three guys share a house. We met at The Village while we were in job training together. We have similar back-grounds. I dropped out of high school. Drifted around aimlessly working dead-end jobs and partying a lot. Got in a scrape with the law and wound up here because the court assigned Ian Montgomery to be my lawyer. This place saved me from a lifetime of bad decisions and introduced me to the Lord."

"That pretty much describes my life, as well." Phil nodded. "Ian was my attorney, too. Mike and I took computer classes here and became good friends. We both love music and computers. Thanks to The Village, we both have fantastic jobs, and we love serving the Lord together."

Luke related a similar story while Brady marveled at how much his life resembled the lives of these guys. He'd never been in trouble with the law, but there were other similarities.

Brady nodded. "Thanks for telling me what The Village has done for you. I'm beginning to see it as more than a place for old folks like my grandmother."

Phil nodded. "We like to tell people about The Village. When we found out about the financial crisis last spring, we did a free concert to help raise money."

"There was a financial crisis at The Village?" Brady narrowed his gaze as he glanced around the table.

"Yeah, the board of directors was ready to close it down, but then everyone rallied around the place and worked to raise funds. We had a huge anonymous donation that really saved this ministry, and now we work really hard to make sure it never happens again." Kirsten's brown eyes appeared misty. "That's why it's so important that the fall festival and the other fundraisers are successes."

"I'm glad I could do my part." Brady swallowed a lump in his throat as he gazed at Kirsten. Was that why she'd been so desperate to contact him? Cora could have been without a place to live. Even if she hadn't sold her house, she wouldn't have been able to live there alone. All this information solidified his decision to stay here for Cora's sake. At least he had the temporary job at the nursing home.

Leslie looked at Kirsten. "What's the status of your visa? We've been praying about it."

"Thanks. I'm still waiting." Kirsten sighed. "Sometimes I think I'll never get back to Brazil, but the mission group I'm a part of has a new work in Costa Rica. They're looking for medical missionaries. I'm considering that option."

Brady's heart sank. "You are?"

"That's *my* plan. I'm beginning to think God may have other plans for me." Kirsten pressed her lips together.

"I'll pray, too." Brady hated to see her sad, but he didn't want her to go. He wasn't going to tell her that he was praying for her to stay right here in Georgia. But if she was that determined to return to the mission field— any mission field—she probably didn't have much interest in starting a relationship with him, despite their upcoming date. Was her resolve to work on a foreign mission field the reason for holding him at arm's length?

Was there any way he could persuade her to change her mind? She had several reasons for not going back. Her work at The Village. Her ties to this group. Her dad. And maybe someday Brady Hewitt, all-around good guy. He could only hope. And pray.

Brady wanted to insinuate himself in to her life, but he could see their goals were far, far apart. He had a lot of work ahead of him if he wanted to change Kirsten's mind about her plans. Maybe he could never accomplish that task. Cooling his pursuit might be the wisest thing he could do for now, but he didn't always choose the wisest path. Besides, he had big plans for their date in two days, and he couldn't back out now.

The cell phone in Kirsten's pocket buzzed as she paced back and forth in her living room. She fished it out of her pocket and looked at the caller ID. Brady. Was he calling to cancel their date? She wasn't sure what to make of the fact that he hadn't mentioned it to anyone. Her dad hadn't asked about it and neither had Cora. So they obviously didn't know. Could Kirsten fault Brady when she hadn't told anyone, either?

She swallowed a lump in her throat before she answered. "Hi, what's going on?"

"I wanted to let you know I'll be a few minutes late. Your dad had car trouble, and I said I'd swing by the campus to take a look. I shouldn't be long."

"Oh, okay. See you in a bit." Kirsten ended the call, her heart racing. Why was she so edgy? Was it the surprise he'd planned or the thought of spending time with Brady…alone? Or was it everything combined—her possible leaving, his less-than-serious attitude and her growing attraction to the man?

For the next twenty minutes, Kirsten continued to pace, stopping every other pass to look out the window. Her stomach churned. She was tying herself in knots over nothing. Taking a deep breath, she finally closed her eyes and said a silent prayer. *Lord, help me to know Your will in my life. Let me put my trust in You and not worry.* As she opened her eyes, the doorbell rang. Despite her prayer, her stomach lurched as she hurried to answer.

Dressed in blue jeans and a long-sleeved rugby shirt, Brady stood at the front door. Charming. Appealing. Disarming.

"Hey, I finally made it." His signature grin lit up his

face. "Glad to see you followed my instructions—jeans and jacket."

"Yeah, I always follow instructions." She smiled despite her stewing insides. She stepped aside and motioned toward the interior of her apartment.

"Got something to take photos with?"

"The phone in my purse." Kirsten wondered what kind of a date required photos. She had no clue. "Do you want to come in?"

"There's no reason if you're ready to go."

"I'm ready." She grabbed her purse and jacket, a nervous energy flowing through her body. What was she supposed to be ready for?

"Super. Let's go." When they reached the parking lot, Brady opened the door to his pickup, and Kirsten hopped inside. The interior sparkled as much as the outside. Had he detailed it just for this date?

Brady turned onto the main road. "Hope this traffic doesn't get worse."

"It probably will. Friday afternoon, and everyone's headed out for the weekend."

Brady turned to her with a grimace. "Guess I shouldn't have stopped to look at your dad's car."

"Did you get it fixed?"

Brady shook his head. "It needs more than I can do."

"You should convince him to buy a new one." Kirsten sighed. "I've tried, but he won't listen to me. Maybe he'll listen to you."

Brady laughed halfheartedly. "Your dad has a mind of his own, so unless he decides to get a new car, I doubt I could convince him."

"Then make him think it's his idea."

Brady frowned as he gave her a sideways glance. "You must think I have a superior power of persuasion."

"You persuaded me to go out with you."

Brady grinned. "Must be my charm."

"Must be." His charm turned her inside out and upside down. What did this date mean to him? For that matter, what did it mean to her? She didn't have the answer to those questions, and she somehow doubted even after the date was over that she would.

Brady chuckled and pointed to the glove box. "There's something in there for you."

Kirsten opened it and an Atlanta Braves baseball cap fell out. She picked it up. "Does this have something to do with your surprise? Baseball season is over, at least for the Braves."

"It's something you'll be glad you have."

"I'm going to need a baseball cap? What's that supposed to mean?"

"For me to know and you to find out. I hope you're not afraid of heights." Brady winked as he took the entrance to Route 400, going north out of the city.

"Heights. A baseball cap. Where are you taking me?" She shook her head and gave him a questioning look. "We're not going toward Stone Mountain, so you can't be putting me on the cable car. By the way, I hate riding in that thing. I don't like being suspended above the ground by wires."

Brady didn't respond. A muscle worked in his jaw, and his knuckles turned white as he gripped the steering wheel. Her heart thudded as she watched his reaction. Had she ruined his plans with her negative comment? Obviously, he had something planned involving heights. They were headed north—maybe to the North Georgia mountains. They rode for several miles in an uncomfortable silence, the pickup's interior suddenly feeling like a prison.

Should she say something? "Hey, I didn't mean to put a damper on your surprise with my statement."

He didn't look at her. "You don't know what it is, so how could you put a damper on it?"

"I don't mind heights. I just don't like the cable car at Stone Mountain."

Brady shrugged. "If we get where we're going and you don't like it, we'll do something else."

"And where is there?" Kirsten hoped she could guess what he had planned if she knew their destination.

"Cumming." He pointed to his phone lying on the console between them. "Use the maps app and put in the address on the piece of paper under the phone."

"Sure." Kirsten typed in the address, and in a few seconds the female voice gave them instructions. Even knowing they were going to Cumming was no clue at all. He wasn't going to say anything else, so she might as well quit guessing and enjoy the ride.

By the time they reached the outskirts of Cumming, Kirsten had made peace with herself about today's outing. She would enjoy whatever Brady had planned. When the voice on the GPS said they'd reached their destination, Kirsten knew exactly what lay ahead and why Brady had asked her about heights.

He pulled to a stop in a parking lot near an open field. Flamboyant fabric lay across the ground as if a huge rainbow had fallen from the sky. Kirsten looked at him. "You're taking me on a hot-air balloon ride."

A sad smile curved his lips when he looked at her. "If you want to go."

"If I want to go? Absolutely."

A little frown creased his brow. "But you said you didn't like to dangle from wires above the ground."

"I've never been on a balloon ride. I think it'll be fun."

"I don't understand it, but I won't question it." He got out of his pickup. "Don't forget your cap. It helps keep your head from getting too hot under the burners."

After pulling her hair back in a ponytail, Kirsten donned the baseball cap and jacket before she went with Brady to the area where they were filling the balloon with hot air. Two other couples waited in the grassy field while the crew worked to ready the balloon. Brady shook hands with the men, and everyone introduced themselves.

Leave it to Brady to think of something like this for their date. Nothing mundane for this man. His worry that she wouldn't like this adventure touched her heart.

Her anticipation grew as the balloon inflated. The basket that would carry them lay on its side while the burner filled the material with hot air. The heat coming from the blast of fire created a sharp contrast to the crisp air of a late-fall afternoon.

The balloon became fuller and slowly rose from the ground like a colorful behemoth awakening from sleep. When the orb was nearly floating vertically above the ground, the crew brought the attached basket to an upright position.

Minutes later, Brady and Kirsten joined the other couples and the pilot in the basket. He looked at them. "Ready for your adventure?"

While the others voiced their readiness, Kirsten only nodded, her stomach roiling from pure expectation. Or was it the thought of dangling above the earth secured only by cables? She looked over at Brady with a tentative smile.

Brady put an arm around her shoulders and leaned close. "Don't look so nervous."

Her heart raced in time to her roiling stomach. "Who's nervous?"

"Maybe you?" His laughter was drowned out by the *whoosh, whoosh, whoosh* of the fire coming from the burner as the multicolored balloon ascended into the canopy of blue.

The pilot motioned toward the road on the left side. "The guys'll be chasing us. They're in that black van you can see in the distance. We'll keep in touch, so they'll be there to pick us up when we land and help gather in the balloon."

"Where do we land?" Kirsten couldn't imagine how the pilot could land this thing.

"We'll find an open space somewhere out there." The pilot looked at Kirsten. "First balloon ride?"

"How'd you know?" She looked at Brady, then back at the pilot.

"The white-knuckle grip on the edge of the basket." The pilot smiled.

Kirsten glanced down to where she was holding on. For sure. White knuckles. She let go and raised her hands above her head. "Look, Ma, no hands."

Brady reached up and grabbed one of her hands and brought it down to her side. He didn't let go. "Don't get too brave."

"I won't." She liked the feel of her hand in his. Her heart did a little flip-flop as she gazed into his eyes.

A murmur of approval came from the other couples, who had each staked out a spot on the edge of the basket. Kirsten remained quiet while they floated over Cumming, the cars, buildings and houses looking like toys. Eventually, the winds took the balloon over the countryside where highways snaked through the forested hills north of Atlanta. They floated over subdivisions with winding streets nestled among the trees.

The breathtaking sights left everyone speechless. The

firing of the burners was the only sound as the balloon drifted silently above the trees.

"Look off to your right." Pointing, the pilot drew everyone's attention. "That's Lake Lanier. And in the distance, you can see the North Georgia mountains."

Kirsten smiled at Brady. "This is more beautiful than I ever imagined. Thanks for the experience."

"You're welcome." He squeezed her hand.

The constant whooshing of the burners made prolonged conversation difficult. For much of the ride, all the occupants in the basket snapped photos and said little as they took in the spectacular views of the surrounding countryside.

Kirsten and Brady stood there wordlessly, hand in hand, as the balloon floated toward the lake. Their fellow travelers also watched in reverent silence as the sun hovered above the horizon like a golden ball, its beams chasing the clouds. The lake served as a giant mirror, reflecting the sun, as the pilot let the balloon descend closer and closer to the water. Then with multiple blasts of the burner, the balloon quickly ascended while it crossed the rest of the lake.

After the balloon was once again over forested terrain, they went higher and higher until they were floating among the clouds. Oranges and golds painted the horizon while the sun sank lower in the sky. Amazed by the spectacle, Kirsten could only marvel at God's creation. Brady had made this trip possible.

Kirsten gazed up at him. "This is almost indescribable."

He let go of her hand and put an arm around her shoulders as he drew her close. "I'm glad we can share this together."

"Me, too." Should she let her heart live a little? She

shook the question away. She didn't have to make any decisions about Brady. All she had to do was enjoy this ride.

Live for right now.

Thinking about the future was off-limits.

While the balloon raced over the treetops, the pilot pointed to a distant field. "We've got a good spot up ahead where we can land, and the winds are taking us at about the right speed."

Kirsten could hardly believe the ride was going to be over so soon. How could that be? She pulled her phone from her pocket and looked at the time. Sure enough, they'd been aloft for nearly an hour—an hour of incredible scenery with a guy she was beginning to care about a whole lot more than she had ever expected.

As they descended toward the field, Kirsten wished the ride never had to end. The sights were extraordinary, but enjoying them with Brady was even more remarkable. Thankfully, the end of the balloon ride wasn't the end of the evening.

"Hold on for the landing," the pilot yelled as they came closer and closer to the ground.

Kirsten grabbed the edge while Brady tightened his hold around her shoulders. His presence spelled security—another surprising thought. When they touched down in a grassy field, the basket skidded along the ground until it came to a stop. The crew that'd been following them raced across the field to help as the mountain of colorful fabric melted to the ground.

Kirsten looked over at Brady and put one hand over her heart. "That was amazing."

"So my surprise was a hit." He gave her a lopsided grin.

"Yes. Thank you." Kirsten turned to the pilot. "And thank you for such a marvelous ride."

"My pleasure. Let us know when you want to go up

again. We're at your service." The pilot busied himself as they folded the fabric in order to get it inside its container. On the way back to Cumming, Brady and Kirsten chatted with the other passengers, crew and pilot. After they got back to the starting point, Brady and Kirsten said goodbye to their fellow voyagers, then headed for Brady's pickup.

Walking across the field, he glanced over at Kirsten. "Ready for something to eat?"

"I am. Is our destination for dinner a surprise, too?"

Brady shook his head. "I'm taking you to a place back down the road specializing in old-fashioned Southern cooking. Fried chicken, fried okra, chicken fried steak and grits."

"You forgot fried green tomatoes."

"I hope you're a fan of Southern cooking."

"I'd say I have to be a fan of fried food."

"Is that a problem?" The same look of concern she'd seen when he'd asked her about heights clouded his features.

"If the food's as good as the balloon ride, there won't be a problem."

"Good." The worry faded from his eyes. "Of course, even if you didn't like the food, you'll like the company."

Kirsten laughed. "Of course. With you, there is never a dull moment."

Brady grinned. "I'm glad you have that figured out."

Did she really have anything figured out where Brady was concerned? She'd promised herself she wasn't going to try to figure out anything tonight, but the question hung over her like the darkness that had settled over Cumming. Being with Brady made her feel like the kaleidoscope of colors coming from the neon signs along the roadway as they drove out of town. Above them a crescent moon chased the stars in and out of the clouds. The night was made for romance.

Keep it light. Keep it in the present. Keep it uncomplicated.

Chapter Eleven

The headlights of his pickup pierced the darkness as Brady turned onto the main highway heading south. He glanced at Kirsten, who seemed lost in thought.

He was a pile of nerves tonight. He didn't know why. Sure he did. He just didn't want to admit it. He wanted Kirsten to love every minute of this date—to love every minute with him. She'd enjoyed the balloon ride, but she would have done that whether he'd been there or not. Dinner was the test, when they actually had to sit down and talk and get to know each other. Would she like Brady Hewitt, warts and all?

When they arrived at the restaurant, Brady breathed a sigh of relief when they didn't have to wait for a table. They studied the menu in silence until the waitress took their drink orders.

When the waitress returned with their drinks, Brady looked over at Kirsten. "You know what you want?"

She didn't answer immediately and looked at him as if he'd asked her a strange question. Then she looked back at the menu. "I think so, but I need another minute to decide."

As the waitress said she'd come back in a few minutes,

he worried there was nothing on the menu that Kirsten liked. He had to quit agonizing over her actions. He couldn't do anything to change the menu. "So what are you thinking?"

Again she was slow to answer. "I can't decide between the fried chicken and the pan-fried trout. What do you think?"

Relief washed over him. So she wasn't concerned about the meal choices. "One of us should order the chicken and the other one order the trout. Then we can share."

Kirsten nodded. "Good idea. I'm also ordering the fried green tomatoes, but I'm not sure I care to share those."

"Whatever you want." Brady chuckled as he closed his menu.

The waitress appeared as if on cue and took their order. While they waited for their food, they fell into an easy conversation. Brady talked about growing up with Cora and how she'd cooked in this same Southern fashion. "That's why I brought you here, so we could have some old-time Southern cooking."

"I got the impression from things you've said before that you really didn't like living in Georgia."

Brady gave her a wry smile. "For the most part that's true, but some things—like Cora's cooking—I made an exception for."

"Anything else you liked?"

Brady shrugged. Was there anything else? Not much, but strangely enough his thoughts about Georgia were changing. "I don't know, but my dislike of the place is slowly waning. You might have something to do with that. I'm sure to have a more positive view if you were going to be here permanently."

Kirsten didn't say anything, but her eyes lit up with a smile. "Are you campaigning to keep me in Georgia?"

"What can I say that will keep you here?"

Silent again, Kirsten lowered her gaze, then finally looked up at him. "It's not about what anyone says. My dad's been telling me I should stay here, too, but I feel like I have a calling to use my nursing skills in areas where medical workers are few and far between."

"And that's a noble thought, but maybe your difficulty in getting a new visa is a sign that you're not supposed to go back."

Kirsten nodded. "I've considered that, but there are other opportunities in other countries. I want to go back to Brazil. That's where my heart is, but the mission group I'm associated with has other missions where I can work in places that don't require visas."

"So does that mean you intend to leave no matter what?"

Kirsten shook her head. "I didn't say that. I'm trying to leave it all in God's hands, but that's hard to do when I want to return."

Brady nodded. "That's how I feel about staying in Georgia to care for Cora."

"Your grandmother's such a love." Kirsten's smile made his heart trip.

"I know." Every time he thought about how he had neglected Cora, his heart ached. "I wish I'd realized when I was a kid. She sacrificed a lot to take me in."

"She probably didn't look at it as a sacrifice at all. She loves you."

Even when he hadn't been very loveable. That's the way God's love was, too. "And I'm grateful."

As he opened his mouth to say something more, the servers brought their orders. Wanting to show Kirsten his faith, Brady took the lead and said a prayer of thanks-giving for their food. Was that good—praying to impress a woman? He was one messed-up dude, but God understood.

Brady looked up after finishing his prayer. "How do you want to share?"

"I'll put some of mine on your plate, and you can put some of yours on mine."

"Works for me." Brady stabbed a piece of chicken and placed it on Kirsten's plate while she put a fish fillet on his.

Kirsten took a bite of her fried green tomatoes. "Mmm, this is so good. Almost as good as the balloon ride. The next time I take a balloon ride, I'll get an order of these to go and combine the two experiences."

"I hope I'm there to see it." Brady held his breath as he waited for her response.

"I doubt there'll be a next time. A balloon ride is a once-in-a-lifetime experience. Thanks for giving me mine."

"You're welcome." Brady didn't say anything else. He'd gladly pay for her to go another time just so he could be with her and see her joy.

"Tell me about your experiences in Alaska. I've always wanted to go there."

"Sure." Her inquiry about his life wrapped his heart with hope. She cared enough to ask about what he'd done in the past. Fishing was something he would gladly share, but he never wanted to go into his time in the army. While they ate, he recounted some of his adventures at sea.

Kirsten set down her fork. "What's your favorite thing about Alaska?"

"The scenery's fantastic—the little of it I had a chance to see. I spent most of my time there on a fishing boat.

Just like you, someday I want to go back and be a tourist. I'd love to take Cora. I hope she'll be well enough soon." Flashes of glaciers and mountains crossed Brady's mind.

"You could go on one of those Alaskan cruises. My grandparents loved theirs."

"That sounds like a good idea." Brady nodded. "Now that I've told you about Alaska, tell me about Brazil."

Her face brightened as if he'd asked her tell him about an old friend—someone very dear to her. He wished she'd look like that when she thought about him. And yet, a hint of sadness hovered at the corners of her mouth. She missed Brazil. How could he think of wishing she couldn't go back?

"Brazil is a beautiful country, almost as big as the US, but most of the people live within two hundred miles of the Atlantic Ocean. So the interior of the country is much less populated. The culture there is very diverse, much like the US." Her eyes held a far-off look.

"Where'd you work?"

"The mission base was near São Paulo in southeastern Brazil. We worked mostly with the poor people who live in the areas ringing the city. Lots of kids on the streets. It's so sad. I had planned to adopt three children who attended our mission classes in São Paulo, but that can't happen now." With tears welling in her eyes, Kirsten touched the beaded bracelet on her left wrist. He'd never seen her without it. "Luciana, Nathalia and Rafael made this for me."

"I'm so sorry that things didn't work out for you and those children. I understand better why you want to go back." He wished he could take away her hurt. He wished she could stay here. He wished she could be a part of his life. Could he make any of those things happen, or was he wishing for the impossible?

"Would you like to go back to any of the places you've lived?" She tried to smile as she blinked back the tears.

Would he? He'd never felt the need to settle anywhere until now. "After leaving Georgia, I never put down roots anywhere. The last place I wanted to be was here."

"Because you don't like the closed-in feeling?"

Brady nodded. She remembered what he'd said before. "But I know now that Cora needs me, and Zach and Tyler need me, too. I have to stay."

"Do you know when you have your foster-parent training?"

"In two weeks when I have another weekend off."

"When you're official, I can make *moqueca* to celebrate."

"That would be great. Thanks." Brady wondered whether making the dish would make her sad. He hated the thought that his joy would cause her sorrow.

"You're going to be a very busy person with school, foster training, work, praise band and watching two kids."

Brady took a big gulp of his water while he thought about all he'd undertaken. "But I won't be too busy to spend time with you."

Kirsten gave him a wry smile. "That's a relief."

"That's good to hear. I wouldn't want you to feel neglected."

Kirsten reached across the table and touched his arm. "I just want to tell you what a special person you are. I'm sorry I gave you a hard time when you first arrived at The Village."

Brady drank in the compliment and her apology, realizing that when he stopped thinking about himself, and thought of others, good things happened. "Thanks. I appreciate your saying that and for letting me discover your heart of gold."

Kirsten laughed. "I'm glad you found it."

During the rest of the dinner and the ride home, their conversation revolved around the success of the festival, Cora's improving health and how much Cora loved having Brady work at the nursing home. By the time he brought his pickup to a stop in front of Kirsten's apartment, he'd come to know a lot more about her. But that knowledge didn't put much hope in his heart that he could find a place in her life, even though her apology and compliments showed that she obviously was beginning to like him.

Brady walked Kirsten to the door, his thoughts now on kissing her. They had shared a wonderful time together, but he didn't want the goodwill he'd established to disappear if he kissed her. Before he'd become a Christian he'd never given a second thought to being with a woman he'd just met. Now he was worried about one kiss.

When they reached the door of her town-house apartment, she fumbled in her purse for her key, finally producing it with a triumphant smile. He swallowed hard as he wondered about his next move. Before he could make a decision, she turned and unlocked her door. It swung open. Suddenly she was silhouetted against the light she'd left on inside, and he couldn't read her expression.

She took one step toward the door. "Thanks for the marvelous day, especially the balloon ride."

"You're welcome. I had a great time, too." How lame. Why couldn't he think of something witty to say?

While he stood there captured by indecision, Kirsten planted a kiss on his cheek and ducked inside. "Thanks again. Good night."

"Good night." His response was lost in the closing of the door.

Some impression he'd made, standing there like an

automaton. He sprinted to his pickup. Putting his head on the steering wheel, he wondered what was happening to him. Maybe it had been too long since he'd been on a date. More likely he'd never been on a date with someone he actually cared about—someone he wanted to impress.

Carrying his guitar, Brady hurried across the quad toward the chapel. With Tyler and Zach in their Friday-afternoon youth group meeting, Brady had just enough time to get in a little practice with the sound system before he sang on Sunday. Sunlight still shone through the stained glass windows on the left side of the chapel as Brady made his way toward the front, his footsteps quiet on the carpeted aisle.

Lost in his thoughts as he moseyed toward the platform, Brady stopped when he realized someone somewhere was crying. A sob resonated high into the arched ceiling. He jerked his head as he tried to figure out where the sound was coming from. Despite the sunlight, dark pockets enveloped the pews on the right side.

Squinting into the dim light, Brady finally spotted Kirsten as she sat in the second pew with her head bowed, her shoulders shaking as she sobbed. Her dark brown hair hung like a curtain around her face. Why was she crying?

His pulse pounded in his head as he stood there, wondering what to do. Should he quietly leave or find out what was troubling her? Maybe she wanted to be alone and didn't want to be disturbed, but every instinct told him he couldn't leave without talking to her.

"Kirsten?" Her name sounded loud in the quiet church, even though he'd whispered it.

She looked up, tears running down her face. She didn't say anything as she stared at him. She wiped away the tears with one hand, then closed her eyes as if she was trying to block out his presence.

"Do you want me to leave?" Brady held his breath.

Shaking her head, she pressed her lips together and didn't say anything. Would she tell him what was wrong? She looked as though speaking would bring her to tears again. His heart in his throat, he swallowed hard as he moved into the pew and sat down beside her. They both sat in silence. Brady wasn't sure what to say now, and Kirsten obviously wasn't ready to talk. He closed his eyes and prayed for her comfort and the right words to say. Her occasional sniffle was the only sound in the cavernous quiet.

After he finished praying, he looked over at her. "Do you want to tell me what's wrong?"

Kirsten nodded, but still seemed unable to speak. She sniffled and wiped at her eyes again. "I'm sorry I'm such a mess."

"You're not a mess. Just tell me what happened."

She licked her lips. "They've made a final decision on my visa request. Denied."

Brady's stomach sank. Bad news for her. Good news for him. How could he be sympathetic when inside he was cheering? If he said he was sorry, he'd be lying. "That's tough news. So does that mean you won't have a chance to go back to Brazil?"

She took a shaky breath, then put a hand over her mouth. Again, she didn't say anything. She closed her eyes for a minute. When she opened them again, she took a deep breath and let it out slowly. "I have to recognize that God is telling me He doesn't want me to go back. That's not what I wanted to hear, but I have to accept it."

Brady wished the joy he felt at hearing her news wasn't caused by something that obviously made her so sad. He wanted her to be happy most of all. Her tears hurt him deep inside. He needed to make her smile. "Guess you're stuck hanging out with me. God knew I needed a missionary in my life."

A smile slipped past her tears as she looked at him. "Are you ever serious?"

Serious about you. He didn't dare say it. "I can be. And now you'll be around to see my serious side."

She smiled again, and his heart soared. She took a deep breath, then let out a heavy sigh. "Even though I've said it over and over how much I wanted to go back, I didn't know how important it was until I found out I couldn't." Sniffling, she wiped another tear away with the back of her hand. "I'm sorry I can't stop crying. When I think about all that's lost, I can't help it."

"It's okay." Brady wanted to pull her into his arms and comfort her. Did he dare? Would she resist? He didn't want her to feel worse than she already did. The take-away from their date and their movie nights left him feeling she'd had a good time, but nothing more would come of it. So he didn't want to overstep and do something to alienate her.

"No it's not. I need to get a hold of myself. It's kind of embarrassing to have you see me like this." She sniffed again.

"I kind of like seeing your human side."

She frowned and smiled at the same time. "There you go again. Trying to make me laugh."

"Glad to see it's working."

"Yeah, you're making me feel better, but I wish I knew for sure where God was leading me. When I went to Brazil, I was so sure of my purpose." She shook her head. "With this development, where is He leading me now?"

Into my arms. Again Brady couldn't say what he was

thinking out loud. She was hurting, and that was probably the last thing she wanted to hear. He was seeing more and more how God could use the circumstances in a person's life to lead them in a new direction. The misfortune of Cora's broken hip had brought him back to Georgia and in contact with Kirsten. The denial of her visa would keep her here. Could he hope God had planned for them to be together?

He sat there for a moment and wondered what had happened to the man who'd gone to war, worked on oil rigs and rode the high seas on a fishing boat? He should be able to tell her how much he cared about her, but the words wouldn't come. How had he become such a coward in the wake of a pretty woman's sorrow?

Brady picked up his guitar. "I came here to practice my song for Sunday, but maybe God brought me here just at the right time, so you could hear it."

Kirsten sat forward and grabbed hold of the back of the pew in front of her. "Because I couldn't make practice this week? Is this something new you've worked on?"

"Yeah, it's something Mike asked me to sing." Brady walked to the back and turned on the sound equipment, then loped to the front and hopped up on the platform. He plugged in his guitar, played a few chords, then quickly tuned it. He prayed the message of the song would lighten Kirsten's heart.

Brady played the opening chords as he looked out at Kirsten, whose smile made his heart trip. Surprisingly, he wasn't nervous as he belted out the words to "My Lighthouse," a song about God's love and peace leading one through the troubles in life. Before it was over, Kirsten was bobbing her head to the catchy tune.

When he finished, she stood up and clapped. "Just what I needed to hear. Please sing it for me again."

"Sure." Brady went through the song again, feeling more confident with every note.

This time when he finished, she came up on the platform with him. "I think you're the missionary in my life. Thank you."

"You're welcome." Brady swallowed hard as he set his guitar in the stand. His breath caught in his throat. They stared into each other's eyes. She was so near that he could easily put his arms around her and pull her close for a kiss. He wasn't going to chicken out this time.

His heart beating faster than he could strum his guitar, he leaned closer. She didn't back away. He put his arms around her waist and pulled her to him. Their lips met, and he was home. He'd been searching for a place to be his whole life, and he'd found it in Kirsten's arms. When the kiss ended she stayed in the circle of his arms with her head against his shoulder.

He'd been brave enough to finally kiss Kirsten, but would he be brave enough to tell her how much he cared about her? Was it too soon? Did he really deserve a woman like Kirsten? The questions raced through his mind, undermining his confidence as he held her. He wouldn't think about them tonight. He would think about this one good thing—their kiss.

When she stepped away, he held her at arm's length. He was falling in love. "That was amazing."

His heart thundered when Kirsten nodded.

Before she could say anything, he blurted, "You want to come over for a movie night?"

"You just want me for my popcorn."

Grinning, Brady shook his head. "I'll trade in the popcorn for the kisses."

"There'll be two little boys hampering your style."

Brady waggled his eyebrows. "They go to bed right after the movie."

Kirsten's laugh echoed in the high ceiling. "What am I going to do with you?"

Love me. The words lingered in his mind, but he couldn't say them and scare her away. He would win her heart. He would. "Discuss a coming-home party for Cora with me."

Kirsten gave him a knowing look as she nodded. "Is this your version of 'I'll show you my sketches'?"

Brady laughed. "Hardly. I already told you up front I intend to kiss you again."

"That's true. I know exactly where I stand."

Suddenly Brady remembered Zach and Tyler. He glanced at the chapel clock. Being with Kirsten had made him forget the time. "I hate to run, but I'm supposed to pick up the boys. I'm late."

"Go. I'll come over after I go home to change." She waved him away.

He grabbed his guitar and raced down the aisle. Another kiss. Another date. Another chance for love. He wanted those things, but did he deserve them? Did Kirsten know where she stood in his life? He'd have to have the courage to find out.

Chapter Twelve

On the following Monday afternoon, Kirsten hurried down the hallway at the nursing home. Hardly able to contain her excitement, she went into Cora's room. The older woman sat in the chair near her bed.

"Good afternoon." Kirsten smiled.

Cora looked her way. "You sound extra happy. Is that because you've been spending time with my grandson?"

Kirsten stared at Cora. What did she know about her and Brady? Had Brady finally told her about their date? Surely not about that amazing kiss in the chapel or the ones they'd shared on Friday night. Her toes still curled whenever she thought about them. Of course, after church yesterday she and Brady had had lunch together with Cora, her dad and the two boys at the senior-center dining hall. The praise band had played for the seniors. So maybe Cora's statement was innocent. She and Brady had spent a good bit of time together lately.

Had the two of them given off signals that something was going on between them? She had to admit, just looking at him made her heart race. What a change from the first time he'd shown up to visit Cora. She wasn't going to give the older woman any clues about Brady. It was his place to talk to his grandmother.

"I don't know about that, but I do know I have very, very good news for you."

"What?"

"The doc has given orders saying you can go back to your apartment."

Cora raised her hands above her head as unshed tears sparkled in her eyes. "Praise the Lord."

"I thought you'd be excited." Kirsten patted Cora's shoulder.

"When do I get out of here?" Cora put a hand to her mouth, then glanced up at Kirsten. "Sorry. I didn't mean to imply that I don't enjoy your company."

Kirsten laughed. "We all know you've been ready to leave here since the day you arrived."

Cora reached up with one of her gnarled hands and touched Kirsten's arm. "Thank you for all you've done for me. Everyone here has been such a blessing. I know I've been cantankerous from time to time, but that just means I love you."

"We know." Kirsten nodded. "One of the aides will be here in a few minutes to move your things back to your apartment. I'll be back with the wheelchair."

Cora frowned. "I don't need a wheelchair."

"You're probably right, but policy is, just like at the hospital, we transport you from here in a wheelchair." Kirsten tilted her head. "Humor me."

"Oh, all right." Cora let out a loud sigh. "But that's the last time I intend to use that thing."

"Remember. Your walker is your new best friend."

Cora frowned again. "I know, but I don't have to like it."

"Eventually, you'll be ready for a cane."

Cora shook her head. "Guess I have to face the fact that I'm getting old."

"But you're never old in spirit."

"Thank you." Cora grinned.

For the first time, Kirsten realized where Brady had gotten his signature grin—from Cora. Or was she just seeing him and thinking about him in everything she did? While she stood there thinking about the man who had captured her heart, the nurse's aide pushed a luggage cart into the room, and Kirsten went to retrieve the wheelchair that had strangely disappeared from Cora's room. She had probably coerced one of the aides to take it away.

As Kirsten pushed the wheelchair, Brady appeared from around the corner. He smiled and her heart thudded. "Hi, you."

He came up beside her. "How's my favorite nurse?"

"Happy."

"Is that because I'm here?" He blew her a kiss.

She pretended to be annoyed. "Don't get too cocky."

"Who's cocky?"

"Surely not you."

"Never." Brady grinned as they walked down the hallway together.

Kirsten paused just before they got to Cora's room. "Is everything ready?"

"The party's ready to begin the minute you wheel Cora through the door. Her friends are anxiously awaiting her return." He leaned closer and whispered, "If we were someplace else, I'd kiss you."

Butterflies took flight in Kirsten's midsection. "Behave."

He gave her a questioning look. "I am or I would've kissed you."

Shaking her head, Kirsten laughed. "Let's get Cora."

When Kirsten and Brady entered Cora's room, her possessions were already loaded on to the luggage cart, and she was pushing her walker toward the door.

"Brady!" She motioned for him to come over, and she gave him a hug. "I suppose Kirsten has told you the good news."

"She has, and I came to help you get settled. I've clocked out, so let me escort you to your chariot." Brady took Cora's hand.

Cora sighed. "I was hoping you'd forget about it."

"Rules are rules." Kirsten adjusted the footrests as Cora settled on the wheelchair.

Brady picked up her walker. "We'll put this thing on the cart. It'll be ready for you to use when you get back to your apartment."

Cora looked up at Kirsten. "Can I say goodbye to everyone before I go?"

Smiling, Kirsten nodded. "We have a whole contingent of folks waiting to say goodbye. Let's go out and see them."

When Kirsten wheeled Cora into the hall, nurses, nurse's aides, therapists and a host of other support people from the nursing home were there. Tears sprang to Cora's eyes as she hugged every one of them. When she finished, she looked over the group and wagged her finger at them. "I can't thank you enough for all you've done for me, and I expect y'all to come visit me."

Murmurs of agreement filled the hallway as the group bid Cora farewell. Kirsten and Brady gave each other conspiratorial smiles as they pushed Cora through the hall leading to the assisted living center.

When Brady pushed open the double doors going into the dining hall, the group gathered there shouted, "Surprise!"

Cora covered her mouth with her hands as her eyes filled with tears again. She looked back at Brady and Kirsten. "You two have been making plans behind my back."

"And we loved every minute." Brady hugged Cora. "Welcome home, Gram."

Liz and Ruby were first in line to give Cora a hug. All the other residents surged around Cora's wheelchair as they welcomed her. After everyone finished with their greetings, she turned to Brady. "Please get me my walker. I've had enough of sitting in this wheelchair."

Brady saluted but looked at Kirsten for confirmation. His concern for Cora melted Kirsten's heart. He'd completely torn down all her resistance against his charm. The charm that had pushed her away in the beginning now beckoned to her at every turn. She couldn't resist.

Trying not to dwell on their budding relationship, Kirsten went over to check on the refreshments for the party while Brady helped Cora with her walker. A big banner with big block letters saying Welcome Back, Cora hung on the wall over the table holding a large sheet cake.

Satisfied that everything was in order, Kirsten turned to find Cora pushing her walker to the table of honor where a bouquet of flowers and a few small gifts sat. Ruby and Liz joined Cora at the table. After the other residents found seats, Brady offered a prayer of thanksgiving for the refreshments and Cora's good health, then escorted Kirsten to Cora's table. A couple of the cafeteria workers served the cake and drinks while Cora opened her gifts and exclaimed over each one.

With happy conversation swirling around Kirsten, thoughts of her relationship with Brady slipped back into her mind. How could she not think about him when he sat next to her? The way he made the older ladies laugh with his goofy jokes served to remind her how much she cared about him.

"You know what I think, Cora?" Ruby's question interrupted Kirsten's musings. "I think that handsome grandson of yours and this sweet Ms. Kirsten should be the next bride and groom here at The Village."

"I'm pushing for that." Cora chortled.

Although Kirsten was dying to look at Brady to see his reaction to the comment, she didn't dare. Her face burned, and she was sure it was several shades of red. What had brought this discussion about? She hadn't even been around Ruby lately. Had Cora put her friend up to this? Whatever the case, Kirsten had no idea how to get out of this discussion gracefully.

"Hey, wait a minute, ladies." Leaning back in his chair, Brady held up his hands. "You can't go marrying me off. You'd be breaking hearts around the world."

Kirsten finally had the courage to look Brady's way. He winked at her as he reached down and gave her hand a squeeze under the table, telling her, she presumed, to play along.

Returning the squeeze, Kirsten gave Brady a tentative smile before she turned her attention to Cora and her friends. "Besides, I'd be robbing the cradle."

"That way you can raise him up like you want him." Liz chuckled.

"I doubt I can change him." Kirsten looked at Brady with a deadpan expression.

"Yeah, and I'm miserable to live with. Just ask her dad." Brady glanced around the table. "So I think y'all should cool any thoughts of weddings."

"But I love weddings." Cora clapped her hands together.

"Then I know who you should work on. Kirsten's dad."

Brady gave her a speculative look. "He has a lady friend, you know."

"Adam and Debra." Cora nodded. "I like the idea."

Ruby leaned forward. "They can be our next project."

Within seconds the three women had forgotten Brady and Kirsten and started planning ways to get Adam and Debra together. While the older ladies talked, Brady touched Kirsten's arm and motioned with his head for her to follow him as he got up. She followed him to the cake table.

He proceeded to help himself to another piece of cake as he stepped close. "Sorry about that. Cora's been pushing for us to be together since the day I got here. She actually told me to ask you out the day we met."

"She did?" Kirsten chuckled, trying to keep the moment light even though she wondered what Brady's apology meant.

"Seems right from the beginning people were trying to put us together. Jen insisted that I ask you to Ian and Annie's wedding."

Brady grinned. "I wish I'd known. I could've handled two dates."

"I suppose." Kirsten didn't know what to make of this conversation. A sick little feeling wound its way into her heart.

Brady put an arm around her shoulders. "I'll talk to Cora. She needs to know she can't keep pushing people together."

"Okay."

When he stood this close, Kirsten's insides scrambled and her heart raced. She couldn't think straight. What did he mean? Was he putting the brakes on their relationship? They'd spent a lot of time together since their official date. Was she making more of his attention than she should? Was she repeating the past?

She attempted to wrap her mind around the way she was feeling. Why couldn't she let go of her worries or her past? Brady had nothing to do with her heartbreak in college. He might be a charmer, but he wasn't selfish. He had a heart to serve others. He cared about Cora, as well as Zach and Tyler.

But how could she consider a relationship with Brady when she planned to leave? Would that be fair to either of them? And the biggest question of them all, the one that had kept her away from forming any serious relationships—how would he react to the fact that she couldn't have children?

Despite all the good things between her and Brady, this one thing still gave her pause about their relationship going forward. Brady loved kids, as evidenced by his applying to become a foster parent for Zach and Tyler. Brady loved to play games with them—games of every kind. He would want to have kids when he got married. He'd even said as much. She couldn't have children, so adoption had been her plan. Could it be his, or was she wishing for the impossible?

If she encouraged their relationship without telling him, he might feel betrayed when she did. On the other hand, bringing up something like that would make a lot of presumptions about where the relationship was headed. How could she handle this? Maybe she was the one who needed to slow down her interest in this man. Her heart ached at the thought.

So many questions. No answers.

Kirsten had to quit thinking about herself. This was Cora's day, but Cora and her friends were the ones who had put the subject of marriage in the center of Kirsten's thoughts. She didn't want to think about it. Her initial plan to go back to Brazil had made the idea of marriage a moot point. Now she didn't have that to hide behind. Brady's talk today made her believe she'd gotten way ahead of herself—definitely way ahead of where his thoughts were.

"Gram, I need to talk to you." Brady hung some of Cora's things in her closet.

"First come over here. I want to give you a hug." Cora leaned on her walker.

Brady went to his grandmother's side and bent down for her hug. He loved this little woman, but her meddling had embarrassed Kirsten. It had to stop.

"Now what did you want to say?" Cora settled in her lounge chair.

Trying to weigh his words, Brady rested against the counter that separated the kitchenette from the living area. He didn't want to sound angry. "Gram, you and your friends have to quit being matchmakers."

"Why?" Cora frowned. "We enjoy it, and it makes people happy."

Brady gritted his teeth. "You didn't make Kirsten or me happy today with your wedding talk."

Cora hung her head. "But I thought you two were an item."

Brady sat on the couch opposite Cora's chair. "Yeah, but we're not talking about marriage."

Cora looked up. "Are you saying you're not interested in marriage?"

"I didn't say that." Why did his grandmother have to interfere? He didn't want to explain his doubts to her.

"Then why shouldn't I push for you to marry a wonderful woman like Kirsten?"

Brady released a heavy sigh. He might as well be up front about his feelings, or his gram would never stop pressing the issue. "First of all, our relationship, if we choose to have one, should move at our pace, not yours."

Cora shrugged. "I was only trying to help it along."

"We don't need your help. Besides, I'm not sure I'm good enough for Kirsten."

His grandmother stared at him as she shook her head. "I don't believe what I'm hearing from you. Don't you dare sell yourself short."

"I'm not. I'm being realistic."

Cora waved a hand at him. "Hogwash. You're intelligent. You're kind. You're fun. You're a hard worker. And to top it all off, you're handsome. What more could a woman want?"

Brady laughed halfheartedly. "Lots. You're seeing me through the lens of a grandmother's love, so—"

"No *so* about it. That's not just me talking. People tell me all the time what a wonderful grandson I have. They see the good things you do."

He shook his head and rubbed a hand across his forehead. He might as well be talking to the wall. "You don't think they're going to come up to you and tell you what a rotten so-and-so your grandson is, do you?"

Cora flashed him an irritated look. "Well, of course not, but they're not going to say nice things if they weren't true. They would say nothing."

So everyone thought he was wonderful. Did Kirsten? Sometimes he thought so. Like today. Then other times he wasn't sure. Ever since he'd met her, there had been this attraction, then pulling back. He didn't know how to interpret what was going on between them.

Brady's biggest doubt camped out in his mind. Would he turn out like his dad—a man who couldn't handle the bad things that marched into his life? Brady didn't want to face that question, but maybe he needed to.

Weighing the outcome of a discussion about his dad, Brady got up and went over to the window. He looked out at the green of the tall pines mixed with the hardwoods with bare branches reaching heavenward. He couldn't look at his grandmother. "I worry about being like my dad. Kirsten doesn't want a man like that."

"Brady, you are not your father." Cora's voice held certainty. "Maybe you only remember the bad times with him. When you were very small, he was a fun-loving, happy man. He loved you and your mother more than anything. By the time you were old enough to remember him, he was already falling into depression. When your mother died so unexpectedly, he couldn't handle it."

Brady turned back to Cora. "What makes me any different?"

Cora wagged a finger at him. "One very important thing. You have your faith. He didn't. He was lost without a light to guide him through a very dark time. He dropped out of life and never found his way back."

Brady didn't say anything for a moment, his mind filled with the words of the song he'd sung first to Kirsten, and then during church yesterday. He turned to face Cora. "And I'll never be like that?"

"Not if you put your faith in Jesus."

"Sometimes my faith isn't that strong."

"We all have doubts."

"Even you?"

"Especially me." Cora nodded. "When we had our falling out, I doubted myself and I doubted God. How could He allow that to happen? But I decided to trust His goodness and prayed every day for you."

"And I appreciate those prayers more than you know."

Brady wasn't about to tell his grandmother about the decadent life he'd lived after they'd parted ways. He wanted to dwell on the good things.

"I also doubted God when I broke my hip and no one could reach you."

Brady hunkered down next to Cora's chair and took one of her hands in his. "And I'm sorry you had to go through that because of my neglect."

"You're forgiven a thousand times over. What's important is what's happening now. God used all the misfortune to bring us together again. And you found Kirsten."

"Thanks, Gram." Cora's statement echoed his recent thoughts. *The misfortune of Cora's broken hip had brought him back to Georgia and in contact with Kirsten.*

"If you're all settled here, I've got a couple of boys who are expecting me to help them with their homework."

"I'm good. Just remember what I've said. Don't you dare let Kirsten get away for lack of trying."

"I promise I won't." Brady leaned over and gave Cora a kiss on the cheek. "Have a good night."

As Brady let himself out of Cora's apartment, his grandmother's words echoed through his brain. *Don't you dare let Kirsten get away for lack of trying.* Brady Hewitt went after what he wanted. He didn't hang back. First on the agenda to win Kirsten's heart was an old-fashioned notion. He was going to talk to Adam about courting his daughter. He wanted her dad's approval.

During the drive home, Brady prayed. He needed courage to talk to Adam. The thought of this conversation churned his stomach. Brady prayed he wouldn't chicken out. If he wanted Kirsten in his life, he would find the courage to have this all-important talk.

Minutes later, Zach and Tyler nearly tackled Brady when he walked into the house. Their excitement to see him warmed his heart. The idea of adopting these boys became more and more a part of his thinking.

Homework. Games. Dinner. Bedtime. The routine did little to calm Brady's nerves as he contemplated his talk with Adam. When the boys' bedtime prayers were over, Brady followed Adam up the stairs.

Adam turned to Brady when they reached the landing. "I'm thinking we should invite Tony and Rebecca Dunn and other children from their house to Thanksgiving dinner. Cora, too. What do you think?"

"Fine with me. Are we cooking? I've cooked a lot of things, but never a turkey."

Adam chuckled. "I'm sure Kirsten will help. When she was still at home, she always helped her mother with Thanksgiving."

Brady stood there, his tongue stuck in neutral. This was his opening to talk about Kirsten, so why couldn't he get his mouth to move? He released the lump in his throat. "Sir, could I talk to you?"

"Sure." A curious look crossed Adam's face.

Brady took a deep breath, but he couldn't get another word out.

Adam smiled wryly. "Does this have anything to do with you and Kirsten?"

Where to begin? The lump returned to his throat, but Brady managed to nod, then swallowed hard. "Yes, sir."

"What would you like to tell me?"

Kirsten's dad wasn't making this easy. Brady summoned his courage. He could do this. "You may or may not know that Kirsten and I have been seeing a lot of each other. We went out on a date a few weeks ago. I'd like to know I have your blessing to keep seeing your daughter."

Lowering his gaze, Adam rubbed the back of his neck. When he looked back at Brady, concern flooded Adam's eyes. Brady's heart sank. The man wasn't happy about this news. Brady wished he could slink away and pretend he'd never brought up the subject.

Adam nodded. "You're a good Christian man. I've always prayed for Kirsten to find one. What are your intentions?"

"Sir, I care very much for Kirsten, but I'm not sure where our current relationship might take us." Brady's heart thundered. Things weren't as bad as he'd thought. Did he dare mention the *M* word?

"You mean as in marriage?" Obviously Adam liked to get right to the heart of the matter.

"Yes, sir." Brady caught a hint of concern in the older man's eyes.

Adam put a hand on Brady's shoulder. "Let's go into the living room where we can sit down and talk."

"Sure." Brady followed, his heart in his throat. A talk didn't sound promising.

When they were seated facing each other, Adam leaned forward. "Has Kirsten told you about her health issues?"

Brady's stomach sank as he shook his head. "What's wrong?"

"Nothing life threatening." Adam rubbed his chin. "Do you know why she planned to adopt the children in Brazil?"

"She said she wanted to save them from their dire situation." Brady wondered where this discussion was going. "Is there something else?"

"I know Kirsten wouldn't want me to tell you this, but I have to." Adam paused. "She had a condition when she was in college that required several surgeries. They left her unable to have children. That's why she wants to adopt."

Brady let the pronouncement soak into his brain. No children. Is that why she seemed somewhat reluctant to pursue a relationship? "That must be hard for her. She loves children."

"It was hard when it happened, but she's decided to make the best of her circumstances. She was ready to adopt three Brazilian children when they closed foreign adoptions at the same time she came home to be with her ailing mother." Adam grimaced. "That whole situation was pretty hard on Kirsten. I think she's just now getting over it. I thought you should know."

"Are you trying to tell me she doesn't want to get married because of that?" Brady's heart ached for her.

"It's definitely on her mind." Adam shrugged. "What I'm trying to tell you is—"

"Pursuing marriage with Kirsten means having no children of my own."

Adam nodded. "Exactly. I don't want her to suffer more heartache by getting to the point of considering marriage and have you walk away because she can't have children."

"I would never do that."

"Are you sure? Think about it long and hard before you further your relationship with my daughter." Adam gave Brady a no-nonsense look. "I only want Kirsten to find a Christian man who will make her happy."

I'm that man. Brady didn't say it out loud, but the words echoed through his mind. "Sir, I'll think about everything you've said. I want Kirsten to be happy, too."

"I appreciate that." Adam stood. "Now this old man is headed to bed. The weeks since the fire have taken a lot out of me."

"At least the reconstruction is going well."

"It is, and that's a relief. On that note, I'll call it a

night." Adam nodded and went up the stairs to his bedroom, leaving Brady alone with his thoughts.

His grandmother's pep talk. Kirsten's inability to have children. Adam's tentative approval. The information whirled through his mind, but the thought of Zach and Tyler brought them all to a stop. Those little boys wanted a real family. Could he adopt Zach and Tyler? Would Kirsten be willing to take the three of them into her life?

As Brady cautioned himself not to get too far ahead of reality, he sank back into the chair. He bowed his head and prayed for God's guidance and wisdom. Brady wanted Kirsten's love. Was that part of God's plan?

Chapter Thirteen

Delicious smells filled her dad's kitchen as Kirsten took the sweet potatoes out of the oven and covered them with marshmallows, then turned to Rebecca. "Looks like everything's about ready. Thanks for your help."

"Thanks to you and your dad for inviting us." Rebecca smiled, but tears welled in her eyes. "It's good to share this time with all the kids we've been caring for."

"You'll soon be back in your house with a couple of new ones." Kirsten gave Rebecca a hug, then stepped back.

"I'll go check with Tony and Adam," Rebecca said. "The turkey should be about ready to come out."

"So glad Tony volunteered to use your radiant cooker."

"Me, too." Rebecca chuckled. "Makes less work for us. And I'm glad we have Brady to entertain the kids."

"Yeah." Kirsten listened to the sounds coming from the living room as Rebecca went out the back door.

Giggles and high-pitched laughter mixing with the deeper tones of adult male laughter floated from the other room. Brady was just a big kid himself, and she loved him. Over the weeks, his charm, fun-loving nature and caring heart had battered down every wall of resistance she had erected. Yes, she loved him. She finally had the courage to admit it to herself. Could she admit it to him?

The thought scared her because she feared his reaction when he found out about her infertility. She didn't want to see the disappointment in his eyes when he learned that truth. How could she tell him without being presumptuous about where their relationship was headed?

Sometimes she thought about how Brady had become involved in the lives of Zach and Tyler. How did Brady feel about adoption? Whenever that question floated through her mind, she shoved it away. It was like all her other thoughts about Brady. They presumed that his feelings were the same as hers, and despite his attention, she couldn't forget his reaction to his grandmother's talk about marriage.

So the strategy was not to tell Brady about her infertility. She probably shouldn't have continued to date him these past few weeks. It was unfair to both of them, but she couldn't bring herself to say no when he'd asked her to go to the latest kid flick with him and the boys, and a week later to the Christian music concert at Jordan Montgomery's church.

She had let herself fall in love instead of sticking to her plan. She blamed her failure on the denial of her visa, or at least she used that as a rationalization. Well, things were about to change again. The mission group had contacted her about helping with a new clinic in Costa Rica. If she decided to go, she would leave Brady behind and hopefully her feelings for him, as well.

Trying not to listen to Brady's laughter, she put the sweet potatoes under the broiler for a minute to brown the marshmallows.

"The domestic look suits you."

Kirsten jumped at the sound of Brady's voice. "Where did you come from?"

"The living room." He grinned.

"You shouldn't sneak up on a person like that." She set the timer for the sweet potatoes.

He leaned closer. "How about if I kiss you?"

"You shouldn't do that, either. Someone might catch you." *And you'd be breaking my heart more than it's already breaking.*

"You mean I might have to explain to some kid why I'm kissing the cook?" He winked.

As the buzzer went off, she waved him away. "Tell the kids to wash up. Food's almost ready."

Kirsten turned off the broiler as Brady left the room. She took the sweet potatoes out of the oven and tried not to think about what she planned to leave behind. During the next several minutes the kitchen became a scene of chaotic happiness as her dad carved the turkey, and the other adults made the final preparations of the side dishes. When everything was lined up on the counter, buffet-style, Adam gave a prayer of thanksgiving for their meal and many blessings.

Kirsten tried not to watch Brady, who was holding the youngest of the Dunns' charges, as she and Rebecca helped the younger kids with their plates and got them settled at the card table sitting next to the dining room table.

After Kirsten filled her own plate, she returned to the table and found Brady sitting beside the one empty chair. Even though there were no place cards, it seemed everyone expected them to sit beside each other. Was her dad looking at them as a couple? She had never said anything to him about her feelings for Brady. If she didn't talk about them, maybe they would go away. She didn't want to face the possibility of his rejection when he found out she couldn't have children.

While everyone was eating, Adam tapped the side of his glass with a knife. The chiming sound drew everyone's attention. "It's been a tradition in my family ever since I was a little boy to share what we are thankful for. I'll go first. Then Rebecca can be next, and we'll go around the table."

"Do I get a turn?" Tyler waved a hand in the air.

"Of course you get a turn." A slow smile crossed Adam's face. "On second thought, you go first. Then we'll have all the kids, then the adults."

"Super." Tyler bounced in his seat. "I'm thankful for Mr. Tony, Ms. Rebecca, Mr. Brady and Mr. Adam. They make me happy. I just have to say that 'cause it's good to tell people how you feel."

"Thanks, Tyler, for reminding us of that important fact." Adam looked over at Kirsten. "In keeping with that sentiment, I'm thankful for Kirsten, who has been such a support for me during a truly difficult year."

Kirsten nodded. Was she going to get through all this thankfulness without shedding a tear? She was afraid her turn would not make her dad happy, but maybe he would understand. The group continued to eat while they listened as each kid took a turn. The kids were thankful for everything from their house parents to favorite stuffed animals that were rescued from the fire.

Rebecca smiled as she surveyed the group. "Wow! I have so much to be thankful for. We might be here all day if I name everything. I'm most thankful that Tony and I can serve at The Village and have these awesome kids as our family."

Tony went next and made a similar statement and

added his thanks for the progress on the reconstruction of their house.

When Cora's turn came she patted Brady's arm. "I am most thankful for my grandson. He's been a true blessing to me."

Brady put an arm around Cora's shoulders and grinned. "I suppose you think I should say I'm most thankful for you?"

"That would be a good idea." Cora chortled along with everyone else.

"And I always do what you tell me to do." Brady squeezed Cora's shoulders. "I'll get serious now. I am thankful for my gram. She was the one person who never gave up on me. I wouldn't be where I am today without her prayers and support. Thanks, Gram."

Cora's eyes welled with tears. "I'm proud to be your grandmother."

Kirsten took in the exchange between Brady and Cora, her eyes growing misty, too. As everyone looked Kirsten's way, she waved a hand in front of her face and pressed her lips together to regain her composure. "You guys are trying to make me cry."

A collective chuckle rolled through the group as Cora reached across Brady and patted Kirsten's arm. "I'll lend you my hankie."

Kirsten's tears dried up in her laughter. "Cora, you always make me smile."

"You'd better smile. It makes—"

"—people wonder what you're up to." Kirsten laughed with the group as she finished Cora's sentence. "Like Rebecca, I'm thankful for so much, but mostly I'm thankful for the past year with my dad. Now I'm thankful for a new opportunity that's come my way. I've been con-

tacted by my former mission group and asked if I want
to help them open a clinic in Costa Rica."

"You have plans to leave again?" Adam asked, concern
in his voice. "When did you hear about this?"

"Just yesterday. Nothing's set for sure, but it's something I'm considering since I can't go back to Brazil."

"But who will the folks in the nursing home depend
on if you're not there?" Cora frowned.

"Jen's still there and all the other nurses and aides.
I'm only one person."

"But I'll miss you." Concern dripped from Cora's
every word.

"And I'll miss you, too. I'll miss everyone, but if God
wants me to go, I shouldn't dismiss this chance to serve."

A cacophony of voices rose around the table as the
adults and the older kids gave their opinions about what
Kirsten should do. All except Brady. He said nothing.
Kirsten wished he would say something.

The wind pulling at Brady's jacket had come out of
nowhere—just like Kirsten's announcement. He didn't
want to believe it. He didn't want to accept it. With an
aching heart, he helped Cora to his pickup, then put her
walker in the back. As he drove to The Village, he waited
for her lecture about Kirsten, but none came. The silence
in the cab choked him like some unseen monster.

The thought of losing Kirsten left him empty and sick
inside. He'd somehow managed to get through the rest
of the day without letting on that he was miserable. He
hoped she'd be gone when he got back to Adam's house.

"You're not going to let her get away, are you?" Cora's
question shattered the silence.

Brady wondered whether Kirsten wanted to get away.
Was she running away because she didn't want to tell

him she couldn't have children? Brady gave his grandmother a sideways glance. "If God wants her to do this work, who am I to stand in her way?"

"Maybe if she had something to keep her here, she wouldn't go."

Brady gripped the steering wheel tighter. "And what would that be?"

"You. Tell her you don't want her to go. Tell her you love her."

"She's supposed to pick me over doing God's work?"

"God could have work for her to do right here. She might not know it. Did you ever think He might have sent you to show her that?"

"God is going to use me?" Brady laughed halfheartedly. "How am I supposed to know what He wants for Kirsten?"

"Pray. She hasn't made a final decision."

Cora's advice to pray left Brady not knowing what to say. What was God's plan in all of this? Brady didn't want Kirsten to go, but maybe he was being selfish. He wondered how he was supposed to figure this out. He drove on, his mind flashing caution like the yellow light ahead. He pulled to a stop and looked at Cora. "I wish I had your conviction."

"Pray. Then tell her how you feel and see what happens. God will give you a clear answer."

Brady wasn't sure he was ready for the answer. What if Kirsten was meant to leave? He'd be willing to go with her except for Cora. She needed him. He couldn't abandon her now. And what about Zach and Tyler? What did God want for them? Would prayer make the answers to these questions evident?

Chapter Fourteen

Brady. The man's name might as well be tattooed on her heart. Despite her tentative plans to go to a foreign mission field again, she couldn't banish him from her thoughts or her life. She walked beside him as he maneuvered Cora in her wheelchair through the Christmas Village at Stone Mountain Park. Christmas joy radiated from every light and every face while Zach and Tyler frolicked a few feet ahead, their happiness contagious.

Only two days had passed since Thanksgiving, but that time had paralyzed her thinking. Kirsten couldn't go forward, and she couldn't go back, her usual decisiveness a victim of fear. Should she answer the call to the mission field or stay and risk her heart? Would she be foolish to listen to the small voice that kept telling her she shouldn't be afraid to take a chance on Brady?

But Kirsten couldn't forget that the invitation to accompany him on this excursion wasn't personal but was all about getting Cora to use a wheelchair without a fuss. Kirsten didn't want to examine why that disappointed her so much when she was the one who was thinking of leaving this man behind.

She had to face reality. She was running away from her

own feelings. A hollow sensation seized her chest when she thought about not seeing Brady again. Shouldn't that tell her what she should do?

"This is like a wonderland." Cora looked back at Brady. "Thank you for bringing me, and you were right about the wheelchair. Too many people for me to use my walker."

"Glad to know Kirsten could talk some sense into you." Brady grinned.

"Now don't get smart with me, young man." Cora gave Brady an annoyed look.

"Just agreeing with you, Gram."

"I'm glad you listened to our advice." Kirsten patted Cora's shoulder and wished listening to her own heart came as easily.

Cora smiled up at Kirsten. "I so enjoyed the program where they sang all the Christmas songs. What's next?"

"Something Zach and Tyler may find fun. A trip to the top of the mountain on the Skyride." Brady motioned toward the boys, who stopped and turned around at the mention of their names.

"You mean that thing over there?" Zach pointed to the cable cars as they hung suspended above the park.

"Yeah, the cable cars." Brady smiled as he glanced at Kirsten. "What do you think, Kirsten?"

She returned Brady's smile as she remembered their discussion about riding the cable car to the top of the mountain. "The view's spectacular, but I think I'll let you take the boys, and Cora and I will see another show."

Brady laughed. "That doesn't surprise me. You and Cora have fun."

"We will. Where should we meet afterward?" Kirsten took hold of the handles on Cora's wheelchair.

"At the restaurant near the train depot. We'll eat, then

take a ride on the train and see all the lights." Brady held up his phone. "Call me when you're done with the show."

"Okay." Kirsten nodded.

"Cool. We get to ride the train." Tyler's freckled face lit up like one of the nearby Christmas lights. "I've never been on a train or a cable car. This is the best day ever."

Cora smiled. "You boys were so good during the singing. I'm glad you get to do something you'll enjoy more."

"See you later." Kirsten waved as Brady and the boys trotted off, then turned to Cora. "What show would you like to see?"

Cora looked down at her program. "How about this cabaret show that starts in thirty minutes?"

"Perfect. We'll head that way now." Kirsten pushed Cora's wheelchair and cast a glance at the cable car, wondering whether Brady and the boys were already making their way to the top of the mountain. Brady—out of sight, but not out of mind.

Kirsten parked Cora's wheelchair and found a place for them to sit near the front. They sat quietly as the auditorium filled with conversation and laughter. Kirsten was lost in thoughts of Brady. Why couldn't she get him out of her mind?

Cora tapped Kirsten on the arm. "Could I ask you a question?"

"Sure." Kirsten wondered what Cora could possibly want to know.

"You've mentioned wanting to adopt children when you were in Brazil. Have you ever thought about adopting Zach and Tyler?"

Kirsten knew the older woman couldn't read minds, but she was obviously very perceptive. "It's crossed my mind. How did you guess?"

Cora shrugged. "I've seen the longing on your face when you interact with them."

Kirsten sighed. "It wouldn't work if I'm going to Costa Rica."

Cora gave Kirsten a pointed look. "Are you sure that's where God really wants you?"

Why was Cora asking all these questions? Did it have to do with Brady? There he was again, popping into her thoughts. "I don't know. A door closed in Brazil. Why shouldn't I look at this opportunity in Costa Rica as God opening a different door for me?"

"You probably should consider it, but maybe God presented an alternative to make you see what you really want." Cora wagged a finger at Kirsten. "There are a lot of people who don't want to see you go. Your dad, all the folks at the nursing home, the members of the praise band, those two little boys and everyone at The Village, especially me."

Kirsten tried not to frown. Cora had left Brady off the list. What did that mean? "What are you trying to tell me?"

"Just be sure you've weighed all the options before you decide that foreign mission work is the right place for you now."

Kirsten had no chance to respond as the show started. She and Cora laughed and applauded through the performance, which was filled with joy, silliness and Christmas songs of every sort.

The show ended, and Kirsten glanced at Cora, who was still smiling. "I'll call Brady and let him know we're finished."

When Brady answered his phone, Kirsten heard the smile in his voice, and her heart tripped. Did he care if she left? "Hey, we're headed to the train depot. What about you? Did you enjoy dangling by a wire above the ground?"

"The boys loved it, but for me it wasn't the same without you and your white knuckles." Brady chuckled. "See you in a few minutes."

Kirsten let Brady's words warm her heart, but did they mean he didn't want her to leave? She wished she knew. The rest of the evening was filled with laughter and happiness as they enjoyed dinner, the train ride, the Christmas parade, the laser show, and the grand finale with the Christmas angel and snow. The atmosphere of this excursion put Kirsten's thoughts on a path toward family togetherness. She cared about Brady and his grandmother, and the two little boys had captured her heart while they'd stayed at her dad's house.

Maybe her dad and Cora were right. Should she consider adopting Zach and Tyler? She'd refused to answer that question time and time again over the past few weeks. Could Brady fit in to this picture? Had she been wrong to even consider going to the mission field again? What did God really want her to do? How could she find that answer? The questions flashed through her mind like the laser lights at the show.

Brady pushed Cora's wheelchair toward the parking lot as they exited, and the tired boys trudged alongside Kirsten. She took one backward glance at the thousands of lights twinkling against the darkness. She couldn't help thinking about Brady. Again. He made her life brighter like those twinkling lights. She couldn't continue to squash her feelings about him, but she needed to know his feelings, too. She had to be brave enough to tell him she loved him.

While she was lost in her thoughts, Tyler tugged on her arm. She looked down. "Did you want something?"

He nodded. "Can you help us buy a present for Mr. Brady and Mr. Adam?"

"Sure. I'll take you shopping." Kirsten nodded. "What do you want for Christmas?"

The little boy hung his head and kicked at a twig lying on the pathway. "It's something too hard to get."

"What's that?" Kirsten imagined some expensive gadget.

Tyler looked up at her with a wishful expression. "A real family. Someone to adopt me and Zach."

A lump rose in Kirsten's throat as she looked at the child. Was Tyler's wish the answer to all her questions? What else could it be? There certainly was no way anything of that sort could be done by Christmas, but she could start the process. And she could pray. "Tyler, I'll certainly pray about that."

He pouted. "I been praying for a long time, but nothing ever happens."

"Don't give up."

Tyler nodded, but he looked doubtful. Kirsten wanted to take that doubt away and make his wish come true.

During the ride home, no one said much as the radio played Christmas carols. Brady dropped off Cora at her apartment, then headed to Adam's house. Kirsten glanced at the backseat, where Zach and Tyler appeared to be asleep.

Kirsten leaned across the console and whispered, "I think you wore them out."

Nodding, Brady smiled but didn't say anything. When they reached her dad's house, Kirsten helped Brady get two very sleepy boys into bed. Her dad had already turned in for the night, so that boded well for her planned talk with Brady about their relationship. She followed him up the stairs.

Brady stopped in the entryway and turned to her. "Thanks for helping me with Cora and the boys."

"No need to thank me. I had a good time." Kirsten stood there, her heart pounding with nervous energy. She wanted to tell Brady everything she was thinking, but she didn't know how to start.

An awkward silence ensued as he reached into his jacket pocket and pulled out a small package wrapped in gold foil and tied with a shimmery gold ribbon. A muscle worked in his jaw as he held it out to her. "I got you something."

She took the package. "You didn't have to do that."

"I know, but I wanted to." He fidgeted with the zipper on his jacket.

While Kirsten pulled off the ribbon, she wondered why Brady seemed so nervous. Was he afraid she wouldn't like the unexpected gift? After removing the paper, she opened the box. A little glass angel accented with gold sat nestled in the tissue paper. She looked up at Brady, her heart thudding. "How did you know I collected angels for my Christmas tree?"

"A photo your dad showed me." Brady moved closer. "Take it out of the box."

Kirsten threaded a finger through the gold string and lifted the angel. It sparkled in the light. "It's beautiful."

"I got it for you because I want to see it on your Christmas tree this year and next year. I don't want you to leave. The Village is the only mission field you need. Please stay and give us a chance to find out if we work as a couple."

Kirsten set the angel back in the box and prayed that Brady would still feel the same way when she told him about her infertility. She swallowed hard. "I need to tell you something before you think about going forward with our relationship. I can't—"

"Can't have children, and it doesn't make any difference to me."

"How'd you know?" Her eyes widened.

"Your dad." Brady held up a hand. "Don't be angry with him. He told me when I asked his blessing to date you. He only wants your happiness and didn't want you getting hurt."

Kirsten held her breath as she searched his face. "Are you sure you want to pursue our relationship, knowing I can't have children?"

He gathered her in his arms and didn't say anything for a moment, then held her at arm's length. "Absolutely, but I want you to know that a relationship with me means a relationship with—"

"Cora?"

Brady grinned. "Yeah, Cora for sure, but possibly two little boys."

"What are you saying?"

Brady dropped his hands from her arms. "I talked to Ian and Melody the other day about adopting Zach and Tyler. How do you feel about that?"

At his words, the empty place in Kirsten's heart flooded with joy beyond any she had known. Overwhelmed with gladness, she couldn't speak, just nodded her head as tears welled in her eyes.

"I'm taking that as an approval."

Kirsten smiled through her tears. "Yes. Tyler told me tonight that he wanted a family for Christmas."

"Well, he's not going to get one for Christmas, but hopefully that time won't be too far away." Brady released a long sigh. "I can't tell the boys until I know more because there are still lots of hoops to jump through, but with God's help, it will happen."

"I think this is a very selfless thing you are doing. You're going to make those boys so happy."

"Can I make you happy, too? I love you, Kirsten. Please stay here and see what our relationship can be."

"Brady Hewitt, I love you. Everything about you— your kind heart, the way you look after Cora, your smart remarks."

Brady grinned. "I knew you couldn't resist my charm."

Kirsten laughed as Brady pulled her closer and kissed her. A kiss that warmed her heart and curled her toes. She had found the place where she belonged—right here in the circle of Brady's arms. God had helped her see where hope for tomorrow resided.

* * * * *

Dear Reader,

Thank you for reading the second book in my Village of Hope series. I hope you enjoyed revisiting characters from the first book, *Second Chance Reunion*. The Village of Hope is a place that offers second chances of all kinds. Not only did Ian and Annie get their second chance in the first book, but Brady and Kirsten find second chances, as well. Brady gets a second chance to make things right with his grandmother, and Kirsten gets a second chance to have the family she has always wanted. They learn that God can take bad circumstances and make something good.

I enjoy hearing from readers. You can connect with me through my website, merrilleewhren.com, or through my Facebook page, facebook.com/MerrilleeWhren.Author. You can also write to me through the Harlequin Reader Service, P.O. Box 9049, Buffalo, NY 14269-9049.

COMING NEXT MONTH FROM
Love Inspired®

Available August 18, 2015

THE RANCHER'S SECOND CHANCE
Martin's Crossing • by Brenda Minton

When former love Grace Thomas shows up at rancher Brody Martin's door pregnant and in trouble, the handsome cowboy is determined to keep her safe. But can he protect his heart from the woman who once broke it?

THE AMISH BRIDE
Lancaster Courtships • by Emma Miller

Ellen Beachey never thought she'd marry—now she has two prospects! To become the wife and mother she's always longed to be, she'll have to choose between handsome widower Neziah Shetler and his easygoing younger brother, Micah.

LAKESIDE HERO
Men of Millbrook Lake • by Lenora Worth

Returning to Millbrook Lake, former marine Alec Caldwell sets about matching injured veterans with service dogs. After meeting baker Marla Hamilton, he discovers that to heal his own wounds, he'll need the strength of this lovely widow and her adorable daughter.

FALLING FOR THE MOM-TO-BE
Maple Springs • by Jenna Mindel

After learning she's pregnant, widow Annie Marshall turns to her late husband's best friend for help. Soon she realizes that a second chance at happily-ever-after may lie in his arms.

AN ALASKAN WEDDING • by Belle Calhoune
Grace Corbett may be the prettiest woman sheriff Boone Prescott's ever seen, but he quickly recognizes the gorgeous city girl is trouble—for his small town of Love, Alaska, and for his guarded heart.

UNEXPECTED FAMILY • by Jill Kemerer
When Tom Sheffield's ex-wife reveals he has a daughter he's never met, he's ready to embrace fatherhood. But can he forgive the repentant Stephanie for keeping their child a secret in hopes of becoming a forever family?

LICNM0815

REQUEST YOUR FREE BOOKS!

2 FREE INSPIRATIONAL NOVELS

PLUS 2

FREE

MYSTERY GIFTS

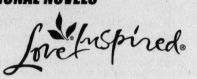

"I'm glad you came for ice cream, Ellen. I wanted to talk to you. Alone," Neziah said.

"*Dat!* Look at me!" Asa cried from the playground.

"I see you!" Neziah waved and looked back at Ellen. "Well, not *exactly* alone," he said wryly.

He continued. "I wanted to talk to you about this whole courting business. First, I want to apologize for my *vadder's*—" He shook his head. "I don't even know what to call it."

"You don't have to apologize, Neziah. My *vadder* was a part of it, too," she told him. "I know our parents mean well, but sometimes it might be better if they didn't get so…*involved*."

He smiled and looked down at his hands. "My father can sometimes be meddlesome, but this time I think our fathers might have a point."

Ellen looked at Neziah, thinking she must have misheard him. "You think…" She just stared at him for a moment in confusion. "You mean you think our fathers have a point in saying it's time we each thought about getting married?"

He met her gaze. He was the same Neziah she had once thought she was in love with, the same warm, dark eyes, but there was something different now. A confidence she hadn't recalled seeing on his plain face.

"Yes. And I think that you and I, Ellen—" he covered her hand with his "—should consider courting again."

Ellen was so shocked, it was a wonder she didn't fall off the picnic table bench. This was the last thing on earth she expected to hear from him. The warmth of his hand on hers made her shiver…and not unpleasantly. She pulled her hand away. "Neziah, I…"

"The past is the past," he said when she couldn't finish her thought. "We were both young then. But we're older now. Wiser. Neither of us is the same stubborn young person we once were." He kept looking at her, his gaze searching hers. "Ellen, I was in love with you once and I think—" he glanced at his boys "—I think I'm still in love with you." He looked back at her. "I *know* I am."

Don't miss
THE AMISH BRIDE by Emma Miller
available September 2015 wherever
Love Inspired® books and ebooks are sold.

"Look at me, Meg," he said in that deep voice. "Who do
you see?"

"What?" She frowned, unsure of what he was doing
and wondering at the sorrow reflected in his eyes.

"Who do you see standing here?"

What did he want from her? she wondered in confusion.

"I see you," she said at last. "Ace Allen."

"If you never believe anything else about me, you can
believe that I would never deliberately harm a hair on
your head."

His statement was much the same as what he'd said the
day before in the woods. It seemed Ace was determined
that she knew he was no threat to her.

"Elton used to stand in the doorway like that a lot.
For just a moment when I looked up I saw him, not you.
I…I'm s-sorry."

"I'm not Elton, Meg."

His voice held an urgency she didn't understand. "I know that."

"Do you?" he persisted. "Look at me. Do I look like Elton?"

"No," she murmured. Elton hadn't been nearly as tall, and unlike Ace he'd been almost too good-looking to be masculine. She'd once heard him called pretty. No one would ever think of Ace Allen as pretty. Striking, surely. Magnificent, maybe. Pretty, never.

"No, and I don't act like him. Can you see that? Do you believe it?"

Still confused, but knowing somehow that her answer was of utmost importance, she whispered, "Yes."

He nodded, and the torment in his eyes faded. "You have nothing to be sorry for, Meg Thomerson. That's something else you can be certain of, so never think it again." With that, he turned and left her alone with her thoughts and a lot of questions.

Don't miss
WOLF CREEK WIDOW by Penny Richards,
available September 2015 wherever
Love Inspired® Historical books and ebooks are sold.

LIHEXP0815